WINTERBAY ABBEY

OTHER BOOKS BY THE AUTHORS
JOHN BLADEK:

Roll Up the Streets!
(Kane Miller, 2010) www.myubam.com/p/1088/roll up the streets

Lost in Ghostville
(Capstone, 2016)

DAVONNA JUROE:

Scarlette: A Paranormal Fairy Tale
(BumbleB Media, Inc., 2012)

Seeing Red
(BumbleB Media, Inc., 2013)

WINTERBAY ABBEY
A GHOST STORY

John Bladek and Davonna Juroe

This story is a work of fiction. Names, characters, places, and incidents are products of the authors' imaginations or used fictitiously. Any resemblance to actual events, locales, or persons, living or dead, is entirely coincidental.

Winterbay Abbey Copyright © 2016 by Davonna Juroe and John Bladek

ISBN-13: 978-0-9973648-0-4

All rights reserved, including the right to reproduce this book or portions thereof in any form without written permission from John Bladek and Davonna Juroe. For inquiries, address Coda Media Ink at, codamediaink@gmail.com

Summary: A Seattle architect travels to a small town in Maine where he becomes entangled in the terrifying past of a menacing ghost haunting an abandoned abbey.

To learn more about author Davonna Juroe, see her website at www.davonnajuroe.com/

To learn more about author John Bladek, see his blog at http://johnbladek.blogspot.com/.

Book cover design, layout, and formatting by Scarlett Rugers Design, www.scarlettrugers.com

Ebook layout and formatting by Jason Anderson, www.polgarusstudio.com

Editing by Jim Whiting, http://jimwhiting.com/

John Bladek and Davonna Juroe author photos © Davonna Juroe
http://www.davonnajuroe.com/

ab·bey

noun

the building or buildings occupied by a community of monks or nuns

CHAPTER ONE

Something felt wrong as I sat down at my desk.

More "wrong," anyway. I loosened my tie.

I was already half an hour late because my car broke down again. After wasting time trying to start it, I had to take my wife Emily's car. Then, as soon as I got into the office, Noelle gave me that I'm-glad-and-sorry-you're-here kind of smile. Something was up, but not enough to account for my prickly anxiety. It went beyond ruffled. It gnawed deep.

Outside the window, the backdrop of gray clouds seemed endless. For over a week now, a constant, silent rain had fallen so lightly you didn't notice until suddenly you were drenched. That definitely was Seattle.

Someone laughed from the narrow aisle between the cubicles behind me.

I turned and glanced over the top of my little cell at the Ikea furniture and plastic plants. Noelle had spilled coffee all over the reception desk and frantically tried to wipe it up with the only thing available—an empty tissue box. Dustin snickered as he watched the scene unfold. He didn't make a move. *I guess Noelle wasn't single enough for him to lend a hand.*

"Here, let me help," I said. I scurried around Dustin to grab a roll of paper towels in the break room and dashed back to wipe up the spilled coffee.

"Thanks," Noelle said. "At least *someone's* a gentleman." She glared at Dustin, smirking over his coffee as he returned to his cubicle. "How's Emily? Did she see that specialist?"

I shook my head. "Insurance won't cover any more physical therapy this year," I said, a lump rising up my throat. "And next year's coverage isn't even that good."

"Sorry," Noelle said. "How's Emily handling it?"

"She's okay, I guess. Thinking more about the baby now."

Noelle smiled. "Only four more months, Dad."

"Four and a half."

Dustin got out his cell phone and loudly put his feet up on his desk. He laughed. "Anyway, sorry, so that blonde I was telling you about…yeah," he said. He leaned back in his chair and continued yet another exaggerated story, this one about a blonde groupie in a miniskirt and glitter, from his ritualistic weekend trips to music venues downtown.

Dustin noticed me watching and flashed an arrogant I-know-something-you-don't-know look followed by another smirk. "It's a great day, isn't it, Larson?" he asked.

"Whatever," I said. "Some of us actually have work to do."

Dustin moved the phone away from his ear. "Why don't you learn how to relax?"

I ground my teeth. It took everything I had to not flip Dustin off. Last week he'd said—behind my back, of course—my latest conceptual sketches looked like Grandpa Simpson had drawn them. I'm sure that got a laugh. Dustin was always the center of attention, especially when he was waiting for you to screw up so he could score points with our boss, Lance.

"What's up with numb-nuts?" I whispered to Noelle.

She shrugged. "I'm not quite sure. He's been giggly since he got here." Her brow furrowed in concern. "You look like a bus ran over your dog. What's wrong?"

I shrugged. "I wish I knew. Must be the weather."

She nodded, and I returned to my desk. A framed photo of Emily, with a smaller, blurry and unidentifiable ultrasound of the baby tucked into the frame, stared back at me. I pushed it aside with a sigh and pulled up my plans for the Greenwood Community Center. Not even Emily's smile could rid me of the sour taste of office politics and jerky co-workers. Creating great buildings was all I wanted to do.

As I paged through my drawings on the computer, I spotted an odd addition. A front exterior elevation sported a pair of windows hovering above the main entrance. The design looked like something out of a 1950s sci-fi movie, and not a good one. They weren't mine.

Dustin snickered again.

I turned around. "Did you do this?" I snapped.

Dustin slowly popped his head over the short wall and locked eyes with me. "Problem?" he asked, putting his hand over his phone.

Heads turned from behind cubicles.

"Damn right," I said. "And you know what it is."

Just then, a sharp ding sounded from my computer. I glanced at the monitor. A message popped up.

Will,

My office. Now.
Lance Graves
Senior Architect
Graves and Sons

As I stared at the message, punching Dustin faded from my thoughts. My shoulder muscles tightened.

Perfect. I needed to fix Dustin's addition before Lance saw the drawings. But there was no time.

Dustin continued smirking. I gave him a last look and got up and headed toward Lance's office, the big corner one across the hall with the view down Phinney Ridge toward Ballard. I tried to not run the worst-case scenario through my head as I knocked on the frosted glass door.

Lance called, "Come in." I opened the door into his private space.

Lance stood near the window holding his cell phone to his ear, reminding me of Dustin. His smile disappeared as soon as he saw my face. Also reminding me of Dustin. He sat down at his custom-welded, steel-gray desk, which matched the frame surrounding a photograph of the Discovery Park Lighthouse.

"Yeah, I got it. Seven o'clock. Yup. Benaroya Hall. I made dinner reservations at Canlis, and I'll pick up my suit during lunch. Don't worry," he said into the phone.

I stared out the window as I waited. A flock of starlings swirled in tight, rhythmic patterns. They moved as one above the traffic.

"There's gas in the Lexus. I have to go." Lance put his phone down. "Sorry. Symphony evening pow-wow," he said.

Sounded rough. Especially as I was spending tonight trying to figure out how to scrape the money together to get my car fixed.

"Why don't you have a seat?" he said.

I sat down in one of his leather chairs. A slight twinge raced up the back of my head. "What's up?" I asked as nonchalantly as I could.

"Look, I'm going to cut right to the chase." He swiveled his computer screen toward me, my drawings on display. "Mark Takamura didn't like the sketches and quite frankly understandably so."

"Sorry, someone hacked my account and made those changes. I've nearly got them fixed."

"What are you talking about?" Lance looked at me like I was wearing a red clown nose and big floppy shoes.

"The windows…over the main entrance?" I said.

He shook his head. "Oh, yeah. I liked those. Why didn't you make the rest of the building match? Did you not hear that the client wanted a modern feel?"

I stared at the drawings. Yeah, I'd heard. The project was an old community center next to the Greenwood Farmers' Market. Originally an elementary school, but now, after several re-purposings, it had been sold to be turned into condos and a restaurant in a mixed residential neighborhood. Mark Takamura's idea was to make the building modern enough that spaceships could land on top of it.

"Well, yeah, but based on the surrounding architecture, I thought maybe a modern look would feel out of place in a building from 1890." I always scoffed at "modern" re-dos of classic structures. Every time I looked at the 1960s "modernist" addition to the Gothic library on the University of Washington campus, I cringed.

Lance sighed. "Will, this business is all about what the client wants. It doesn't matter how ugly or out of place *you* think it looks. That building was never important or unique enough to make it on the historic register. They're free to do whatever they want with it. And remember: they are paying you…." He cleared his throat. "*Us*, and it's our job to make it fit their needs."

"I'm sorry. I'll do it over again," I said. *Note to self: put in a garage for flying cars.*

"Not necessary," Lance said. "I'm handing the account over to Dustin."

A knife blade shot into the back of my head. "What? Hold on. I think that—"

"No, you're too late. Will, when you first came here, I was impressed with your ideas and vision. *That* Will listened to clients and executed what they wanted." Lance tapped his finger on the screen again. "I know every architect dreams of injecting their personality into buildings. You'll get to do that someday, but not now. Business trumps art."

I squeezed my fist. "Sorry. I guess I've been a little distracted lately with Emily. If you just give me another chance to fix things…" I said, ashamed of the pleading in my voice.

Lance checked his watch. "Yeah, well, everyone's had a pregnant wife. Figure out how to listen through your personal distractions and when to give up on wrong ideas. Stop making excuses."

I stared out the window as Lance continued his lecture.

"This is the same thing as the Denny project," he continued. "Getting that simple atrium 'perfect,' *by your standards*, cost us a month."

I could feel his laser glare. This wasn't my first job or the first that had taken a wrong turn. For a second, I thought about resigning, telling Lance I was sick of his micromanaging my work, sick of Dustin and his pranks, sick of working for clients who wanted to turn Seattle into San Francisco.

But the words that came out were far different. "Isn't there *something* I can do to fix the design?" I was pleading before; now I sounded like I should be on my knees.

Lance spun in his chair and looked out the window. "I'm sorry, but maybe you aren't cut out for a firm like this. Too much pressure. You need something less stressful, give you more time to take care of your wife."

"I need a job to do that," I said. "She hasn't been able to work. If you'll just give me one more chance, I promise…."

Lance swiveled back and picked up a file from his desk. I sucked in a breath, expecting him to hand me my severance notice. My head pounded. What was I going to tell Emily? And the mortgage company?

"I'm going to give you one more chance," Lance said.

I blinked, unsure I'd heard him right.

"Over the weekend, I met with two Seattle developers who are looking to convert an old abbey into a hotel. The project is on the coast of Maine. Winterbay. Maybe you've heard of it. I know I haven't." He gave me a slight smile and handed me the folder. "You would leave tomorrow."

"Maine?" I asked. "*Now?*"

"No one else is interested, frankly, or I wouldn't offer it to you. Take it or leave it."

I flipped the folder open to a couple of photos of a weather-beaten building with crumbling brick walls, missing shingles, cracked windows, and a general look of decay and abandonment. The dreary old building brought an even bigger rain cloud down on me.

What choice did I have? "I won't mess up again. I promise."

"We'll see."

I got up to go, hoping we were done.

"I'll see you back here in a week or so," Lance said. "Unless the developers aren't happy."

I didn't ask what would happen then.

"We can't give you the new 3-D hemispheric laser scanner. Dustin needs it. You'll have to get by with the old one."

"Okay," I said. "Thanks for the chance." I let myself out the door, closing it quietly.

My temples throbbed. I reached into my pocket for a bottle of Tylenol and dry-swallowed two pills. A vibrating buzz shook my pocket. I picked up my phone. The caller ID flashed a picture of Emily holding her newest sonogram. I pushed the "decline" button and walked down the hall to arrange my flight.

CHAPTER TWO

The traffic on Greenwood Avenue North on the way home was slow even by Seattle standards. The wind blew leaves in twisting swirls across the road. As the trees swayed in the breeze, the streetlights flickered on while the sunless sky dipped further into darkness.

I had skipped out of work as soon as the clock struck five, otherwise I might have punched Dustin's fat face. I took another look at the Winterbay folder while sitting at an intersection standstill. I didn't have any ideas for it: a rundown wreck of a building in the middle of nowhere. As I scanned the photos, I thought again of quitting, looking for work somewhere else, somewhere I'd be appreciated and treated like a professional.

Who was I kidding?

Maybe I should just quit architecture altogether. It's not like it paid that well, and it was one of the most volatile professions anyway. I should've gone into the tech industry. Almost every single programmer here was driving around in a Tesla.

A motorcycle pulled up next to me, engine revving. I closed my eyes. My head spun. All of a sudden, I was skidding and could hear Emily screaming. *Her hand, oh my God, her hand!*

The car behind me honked and brought me back into the moment. My heart pounded in my ears, and my hands shook on the wheel. I shut the folder and eased forward twenty feet to satisfy the pushy guy behind me. It would be nice if the flashbacks didn't happen every time I heard a motorcycle. I took a long breath, trying to keep my memories from overtaking my emotions.

Traffic stayed slow, and I was glad for the extra mental recovery time. Half an hour later, I finally snailed my way into our tree-lined Broadview neighborhood. The lights were on in our house, creating a warm glow against the dark fall sky. I'd never felt so glad to get home and relax in my recliner. I groaned. I was really starting to sound like my dad.

I pulled into the driveway to the sight of my non-starting car with a gash in the side door. It had never been the same since the accident. I parked and got out to check the mail. A red stamp marked "Final Notice" highlighted a letter from the mortgage company.

I ripped the envelope in half.

I'd have to call them again.

"I thought I heard you pull in!"

I jumped when I saw my wife standing at the door. Emily was wearing overalls, accentuating her growing belly, and her blond hair was pulled back into a tight ponytail. Dark circles outlined her eyes. I hoped she hadn't seen what I'd just done.

"You just missed your mom," Emily said.

"Oh, uh. She was here?" I gave her a hug and tried not to knock over the new planter.

"Yeah, she dropped off some of your childhood keepsakes. Come look at this stuff! It's *soooooo* cute!" she said.

I rolled my eyes. Space was precious in our cramped little house. I'd left my old junk behind at my parents' house for a reason. Probably the same reason they were dumping it here.

The smell of chicken noodle soup filled the air as I crossed the threshold. The TV hummed in the background, reruns of some weird program Emily liked about people contacting dead relatives or something with angels. I never watched it.

In a way, I envied Emily. Staying home all the time sounded nice. Even the thought of being a stay-at-home dad was enticing. Too bad paternity leave was an all-out joke.

I glanced at Emily's dress figures in the living room. Eight months ago they were always out, hung with new designs, sketches spread across her cutting table, pins underfoot. Now they were stuffed into the corner behind a chair, naked and unused.

She caught my eye and I quickly looked back and smiled.

"I had some ideas," she said, "for a new skirt."

I nodded. "That's great."

"But they're still in my head. I'll get to it soon," she said.

I tried to smile again, but couldn't. I wasn't sure she'd ever have the needed dexterity again for any fine work. Emily's hands had once been supple and graceful. Artist hands. They still were, at least one of them, no thanks to me.

"Do you want to see the stuff your mom brought?" Emily led me to the couch. A clear zippered bag sat on the middle cushion. Tiny shoes, bibs, and other infant paraphernalia littered the entire sofa. I recognized a couple of toys.

Did my mom really keep all this?

I was tempted to throw all of it out, but maybe we could reuse the clothes. We certainly weren't going to have the cash for new ones.

"Just look at this," Emily said, holding up a yellow onesie. The shiny, jagged U-shaped scar on her hand caught the reflection from the recessed lighting above. The skin graft that covered the entire back of her hand wasn't as angry now, but I still noticed. It looked like the hand belonged to someone else even though the skin came from her hip. At least it hid the crushed bones and ligaments underneath.

She flexed her fingers. I could see the strain in her face as she barely managed to make a fist.

She put the onesie down and handed me a round rattle topped with a short blue-striped wooden handle.

"Your mom said you were worse than a dog. See those marks." She pointed at the rattle's handle and smiled.

Tiny teeth marks imprinted every inch of the soft wood. The indentations formed an odd pattern of wavy bites. Gross. It did look more like a puppy's chew toy than a baby's rattle. Why had my mom held onto this? "Uh, huh." I walked over to the garbage can and dropped the rattle inside.

Emily's eyes darkened. "You know, the least you could do is act a little bit excited sometimes," she said, rubbing her stomach.

I stared at the toy at the bottom of the garbage can.

"I think all the time about my dad, up there in heaven with the angels, watching over me," she said. "Pretty sure he's looking forward to a grandchild."

I swallowed, and my chest turned cold. At first, I hadn't been excited to hear about the pregnancy. In fact, I'd panicked. Financial fears perched like vultures on my shoulders. Emily and I weren't even close to paying off our student loans, and her injury set us back that much further. The five months I'd been out of work a year and a half ago almost made us hit bottom. I'd told myself that all of that had put a damper on my initial excitement. Was I also afraid to admit that maybe part of me wasn't ready to be a father?

"I'm sorry." I hugged her. "There's been a lot of stress lately. How about I go through the rest of my baby stuff with you, and we can figure out what to keep or throw away?" I bent over and pulled the rattle out of the trash.

"That would be great," she said, brightening. "You can toss that thing, though. It's been well-used." She winked, took the toy from me, and dropped it back in the bin.

I squeezed her. "How was your day?"

"It was good. I found some more shirts for you at the thrift store," she said, beginning to fold my baby clothes.

I faked a smile. The Takamura account was supposed to get me a raise so we could not only buy new shirts but also get a bedroom decorated and ready for the baby.

"Ariel actually came shopping with me," Emily said.

"Oh, really? How's she doing?"

"Still crying a lot." Emily sighed. "At least I was able to get her out of the house. We talked about going to a new gallery in Georgetown that shows fantasy-inspired works. Opening night is free and open to the public. They're supposed to have some awesome steampunk outfits and fairy-fashioned clothes." She dropped her eyes.

Out of everything Emily ever liked to make, costuming was her ultimate joy. Before the accident, she was trying to secure a deal with a local costume shop to buy some of her designs.

"Well, that sounds fun," I said. "Ariel likes fairies. Or maybe that's just you."

"I just wish there was more I could do," she said, looking down at her feet.

"You'll be able to do more someday. Just take it one day at a time right now," I said.

She shook her head, "Yeah, someday. But's that's not what I meant. I meant do more for Ariel."

"Oh," I said. "It's not your fault, Em."

"I know. I know. It's just that she's been so stressed out about her job. If I had just helped her, like, been there for her more. Maybe taken more meals over, then everything would've—"

"Shhhh," I said, putting my arms around her.

She put her head on my shoulder.

"Don't blame yourself. Ariel's miscarriage was bizarre, remember? They usually don't happen in the third trimester. Try to separate yourself from your friends' problems. Everything's going to be okay."

"Yeah, sure," she said, nodding.

"Did you sleep better last night?" I asked.

"I…" Emily said, wiggling her fingers. "Maybe a little."

"Maybe a little" usually meant "no" in Emily's world. Her hand ached at night, and since she'd gotten pregnant, she tended to have frequent nightmares and very little sleep. My leaving town would probably make her insomnia worse. I had kind of hoped Ariel would make things easier if she came and stayed for a bit while I was gone. I didn't want Emily alone, but maybe Ariel was a bad choice to keep her company.

She made her way into the kitchen. "We better have dinner or it will get cold." The sound of clattering dishes followed.

I sat down at our desktop computer. When I moved the mouse the screen lit up. Emily's resume was open. "How's the job search going?" I asked. I went cold every time I saw a resume, thinking of how long I'd posted mine online with no takers until Lance.

She sighed. "Nothing yet. I'm still waiting on Microsoft. They have a new work-from-home posting."

"Anything else? Project management, maybe?" I asked.

Emily frowned. "I'm trying. It's not that easy, you know. It looks like I would need to get some extra training, and it's expensive." She looked down at her hand and tried to wiggle her fingers. They flexed an inch but no more. "I was actually kind of thinking.... Um, maybe this isn't the best time to look for a job."

I spun around. "What? What do you mean?"

"Well, with the baby coming, I don't know if I should be starting a new job. I'll be kind of occupied for a while."

I nodded. I'd known that was what she meant, but I didn't like to hear it.

"I.... Yeah, we just need to get you back on your feet as soon as possible. That's all I'm saying."

She drew in a deep breath. "I want to go back to what I was doing." She flicked her eyes toward the dress forms. "You know, design. I actually thought I would talk to that gallery director in Georgetown about costumes, displays, you know."

My guts clenched. I didn't know what was worse, seeing her uncovered forms that she couldn't sew or even draw for, or hearing her talk about trying to set up something she wasn't capable of doing yet. All because of me.

I nodded. "I want that too, but…"

"I tried knitting today," she said. "You know, that project I told you about. It's coming along nicely. I'll be done soon. Maybe if I could sell some things online…"

"That's great, but does that ever really work? Even if you could make things fast enough, they'd have to sell for a thousand dollars apiece," I said.

"Thanks for the vote of confidence and support," she said, her eyes flaring. She slipped her bad hand under the other arm, hiding it from view.

We both looked away. I felt bad, but I was also trying to be realistic about our situation. An awkward silence formed a cool wall. I hated to admit it, but more and more of these barriers were building. Things just weren't the same between us. Not since the accident.

I used to race home to Emily at the end of my day so we could grab takeout and rent a movie. Our legs would intertwine as we sat on the couch, holding our chopsticks and watching the newest superhero or sci-fi movie. She loved to critique the costumes. In the summer we would walk hand in hand for long strolls in many of Seattle's parks.

I couldn't even remember the last time we watched a movie, or even held hands.

I really wondered if Emily hadn't gotten pregnant—another accident—if she would have already left me. Thinking about it made me feel sick to my stomach. I had tried so hard to do everything I could to make her happy in the eight months since the crash. It felt like all my efforts fell flat.

"Anyway," Emily finally said, her tone chilled, "has Lance told you what Mark thought of your designs yet?"

I rubbed my head. I'd hoped to at least wait to tell her about Maine until after dinner. "Um, yeah."

Emily stared at me. "What?"

I put my hands behind my head and stared at the ceiling. "Apparently Mark thought my CADs weren't quite 'modern enough.' Lance ended up giving the account to Dustin."

Emily dropped an empty bowl and clutched her hand. Luckily the fall wasn't china-fatal. She let out a curse. "*How?!* They were perfect. Modern does *not* even begin to fit that neighborhood," she said.

"I know. It just wasn't what he wanted," I said with a shrug. I explained how Dustin had sabotaged my drawings.

"Will, I'm so sorry. What are you going to do?"

"Well, Lance put me on a different project. But this one involves some traveling," I said, leaving out the part about Lance giving me one last chance to prove myself.

"Really? Where?" she asked.

"East coast. Maine," I said.

Emily's body went rigid. "*Maine?* But—"

"I know it's far," I said.

Emily's face sank. "I feel weird being alone right now, after Ariel…"

I swallowed, not sure what to say. "I know. I thought about quitting, especially with having to go to Maine."

Emily shook her head. "You can't do that, not again. I can't believe you'd even *think* about quitting right now!"

"I know. I know. I'm not going to. I was just telling you what I was thinking. Anyway, could your mom maybe stay while I'm gone?"

"Just forget it," she said, looking away. "I'll be fine. When do you leave?"

"Em…don't…"

"I'll be *fine*."

"Tomorrow," I said. "I leave tomorrow. I'm sorry about all this."

Emily stalked back into the kitchen. "I'm leaving your dinner on the counter."

She hurried toward the bedroom.

After staring into space for a moment, I sat in the recliner.

I didn't bother getting my soup.

CHAPTER THREE

A flash of slick road. Headlight glare. A kid. A motorcycle.
  A high piercing wail that punctures my heart.
  Emily!

I shook my head as Emily merged onto I-5 southbound toward the airport. I grabbed the passenger door grip and took a deep breath. Two flashbacks in two days. Before these recent episodes, I hadn't had one in a month.

I didn't know if the flashbacks worried me more when Emily was driving or when I was. The horror always returned, and the result never changed.

Thankfully, Emily didn't notice my state. She was focused on the road. In fact, she'd been quiet the whole drive. Not even the orange gerbera daisies I'd woken up early to run out and buy for her softened the mood.

After a goodbye hug and cliché promises about staying warm, I made my way toward security with an even fuller stomach of guilt.

Emily's mom was coming to stay with her tomorrow morning. Thankfully, Emily had a change of heart at the last minute and decided to call her. That should have made me feel better. But as soon as I got to my gate, that same strange anxiety I'd felt at the office yesterday crept up my chest. It burrowed in to stay, along with my headaches, which seemed to be getting worse. They say that when you become a parent everything changes. Maybe a little of this was part of some new protective separation anxiety.

Whatever the reason, I didn't like it, and I hoped visions of the accident dancing in my head remained at bay as well. I took out my Tylenol and chewed two pills.

I tried to distract myself during the flight by researching the two Winterbay developers. Ted Alderstone and James Spears were from Seattle. They had restored some old buildings in Belltown into posh condos, complete with rooftop gardens and barely noticeable solar panels. Pretty impressive, even for Belltown. The neighborhood was known for its high crime and sketchy nightclubs, although it had experienced a revamp within the past few years.

I opened the folder Lance had given me and stared at a bell tower looming over the seaside of the abbey. Stately and shabby at the same time, the tower seemed to fade in and out of focus. I rubbed my eyes, wishing I'd gotten more sleep. I hadn't slept well in months and that was probably exacerbating my troubles. I needed my creativity for this renovation and to hone in on the clients' wishes for their new building. But no ideas came to mind. I gazed at the tower. It continued to flicker. I blinked and stifled a yawn.

"Hey, excuse me?" The guy next to me said, tapping my shoulder.

"Yes?" I asked.

"Well, are you getting up or not?" he asked.

"Getting up?" I asked.

I glanced around the airplane. Everyone was standing, grabbing their bags.

"We're here?"

"Yeah. Time flies," he said, shrugging and raising his eyebrows.

How could we be here already? I'd just gotten on the plane. Had I really been looking at this photo the entire trip? That seemed impossible. I must have fallen asleep for hours.

The guy made a move to stand, and I pushed my way out into the aisle. The next couple of hours were a blur. I didn't have much time to think. I had to run to make my connection to a smaller plane, then after getting stuck next to a man who wouldn't shut up for the entire flight, finally landed at the airport nearest Winterbay. It was still an hour's drive away. I grabbed my bag and texted Emily that I was on the ground and would call her soon. It was 9:00 PM local time.

I found my rental car in the dimly lit parking lot. Slush spilled over the tops of my shoes, soaking my feet. Coming from Seattle, snow wasn't something I was used to. If it did snow—which was rare—the entire city shut down. Typically we'd abandon our cars and walk home to watch "Snowmageddon" on the local news. Sometimes, for days. I was sure this was the type of town where people walked barefoot in five feet of snow to get to their destinations.

I typed the address of the hotel into the navigation console. After about twenty minutes of heading north, the highway forked toward the east and my GPS ushered me into the sleepy town. I'd done a quick internet search on Winterbay before leaving. Winterbay's tourism site said it was founded in the 1740s as a fishing and lumber port. The town sat on a small inlet of the large bay for which it was named. Judging from the map, a mile-long spike of rocky ridge jutted into the bay to separate the town from the northern cove, the site of the abbey.

Brick shops lined Main Street, and white lights twinkled in windows. The snow around the stores gave an otherworldly shimmer to the picturesque scene, a still shot from a Hallmark Christmas card. The village looked quaint and exuded a Craftsman-like all-American charm, albeit covered by a cloudy shroud of mid-fall gloom. It looked like just the type of town that could do with a restored hotel. It already had some of the perfect drawing cards for tourists, including a rugged shoreline with beautiful views.

My stomach growled. I'd missed dinner. I pulled into the first place I saw, the Rusty Whale, a tavern with a neon burger flashing in the window. A burger and beer sounded just right.

A couple of red vinyl booths lined the front windows, with several more tables inside. The bar looked more inviting and probably quicker, so I sat there.

I waved to the bartender. "Could I get a burger and something on tap?"

The man, who looked in his thirties with an unkempt beard, ponytail, and pierced eyebrow, gave the overly lacquered bar a quick wipe with a soggy towel and nodded.

"Have your drink right up," he said in a New England accent, sliding a ketchup bottle in front of me. The local brew was called *Winterbay Nor'easter*, a rich, crisp dark ale that gave off the scent of a forest after a rain.

About halfway through my beer, I looked toward the kitchen. I hoped the food wouldn't take much longer. I still needed to check into my hotel, call Emily, and get to bed at a somewhat reasonable hour.

I glanced above the kitchen pass-through window. A painting hung there, a track light illuminating the artwork. The scene showed a high bluff above a stormy sea. Wind whipped a froth of gray waves, and a lone figure walked along the beach as if he was the last man on earth. I stared at the painting, suddenly feeling isolated and alone.

"Hello."

I jumped when an older man next to me waved his hand in front of my face. He wore a black pea coat and had long gray eyebrows. I hadn't even seen him sit down.

What was with me today?

I smiled back as the man and the bartender exchanged glances. A full pint appeared before him. The old man looked at me out of the corner of his eye. His face was thin and had a satyr-like quality.

"Tourist?" he asked, his voice gravelly and harsh.

People here didn't mince words. "Not exactly," I said, turning to face him.

His nose was red from the cold, his eyes watery.

"I'm in town to do some work. Name's Will."

"Martin," he said, holding out a hand that swallowed mine. "What kind of work?"

"Architect. Remodeling the old abbey outside of town."

Martin snorted. "Winterbay Abbey?"

"Yes. Do you know it?"

"The abbey? Sure. Everyone does. Never cared for it. But the bay, now that's a sight."

"Really? Nice views?"

He pointed to the painting above the bar. "That's it, right there. Captured by Arthur Parton in all its glory."

I focused on the artwork again.

"Beautiful. On the surface," he said.

I frowned. "On the surface?"

"Wild place," he said, taking a sip of his drink. "That's why the town was built here. This cove's better protected. The sudden fogs up there are like nothing you've ever seen. One minute you see for a dozen miles, the next you can't find the end of your nose."

I sipped my own warming brew. "Sounds interesting," I said, looking away from the canvas.

He glanced toward the back of the bar, staring at the rows of bottles. Then he sniffed. "The tides can be ferocious. They race out and roar back on the Devil's timetable. Undertow to beat all hell. Makes manning a lighthouse a bit tricky. But the shipwrecks there, now that's where the tales are."

This sounded cool. I loved a good sea tale, especially one that might distract me from my gut-deep loneliness. "So, if the port is here, why are there shipwrecks by the abbey?" I asked.

"Hard to know which cove is which," Martin said. "Too easy to get lost. Bay of Lost Souls, it should be called. Ships by the dozen—fishing scows, whalers, schooners loaded with timber for the British navy back before the Revolution, even a destroyer during WWI, all of them broke their backs on a spit of submerged rocks at the head of the bay. Men drowned by the score for over three hundred years. Winter storms drove them there, that's where the name comes from. Winterbay. Cold, desolate place."

A small hint of a smile crossed his lips as I stared at him. He really was starting to sound like a crusty old pirate.

"That's why there's a lighthouse there, although it wasn't built till a century ago. Men died in droves before then. Cursed, it is."

"That's terrible," I said, although I was still intrigued. "I wonder why I didn't come across those stories in my research."

He shrugged and downed the rest of his beer in one long swallow. After a nod the bartender brought another.

"Here, I'll get that," I offered, setting my credit card on the bar. Or, really what I should have said was, "work will get that."

"Thanks," he said. "Tourist board here likes to keep a happy face, nothing but smiles and ocean views. But shipwrecks still happen to this day, despite the lighthouse and GPS. Some poor drowned soul just recently washed up on shore."

I swallowed another sip of my drink, while unease crept in around the edges of my mind. Drownings did not attract visitors. "Really? When?" I asked.

"About two months ago. Some pleasure boater from Kennebunkport got lost," he replied. "Those rocks I mentioned, Satan's spine, they are. The charts all say Lobster Rocks 'cause they used to get giant lobsters. Been a long time since the bay was played out. Though that's not what the curse is about."

The bartender laughed and shook his head. "Martin trap you here for one of his stories? You might not escape."

I smiled and looked back at Martin. This guy obviously had a reputation of spinning tales. Probably no reason to feel uneasy.

"It started in 1650," he continued, ignoring the bartender. "English ship, the *Damask Rose*, was off the coast, loaded with cod. Storm blew in out of nowhere, pushed the ship into Winterbay. The native Penobscot were there to see, told the tales. Waves as high as the spars swept the *Rose*. The Penobscot were skilled sailors, and they made the coastal fisheries hell for English ships, even capturing some and using them against the English. But the storm was too severe even for them. They watched, waiting for the wind to blow the *Rose* onto the rocks.

"Then the wind shifted, and the *Rose* appeared to be saved. But just as it seemed about to escape, a blue glow surrounded her. Terrible cries rose up even in the teeth of the howling wind, of men driven mad. All hands lost but one. Cabin boy. The lad washed ashore, barely alive, and the natives took him in, raised him as their own until an English raiding party captured him back. He spoke of a siren's song that called the ship to the rocks. Ever since, sailors tell tales of seeing the ghosts of the *Rose*, beckoning them to their deaths."

I caught the bartender rolling his eyes.

"Ghosts?" I said to Martin. I heard plenty of ghost stories from Emily, and I had trouble pretending I believed them. I usually gave her the same look I gave Lance when he suggested I listen to ridiculous ideas of clients who wouldn't know a good design if it landed on their heads.

My burger showed up, and I poured ketchup on the fries. Martin eyed them longingly. He looked away when I caught his eye. "Can I get you something to eat?" I offered. The Graves and Sons' business expense account could use more charging tonight.

His eyes lit up.

I motioned for the bartender. "Burger?" I asked.

He nodded.

"So tell me more," I said.

Martin went on. "That was just the first story. More ships were wrecked in the bay. Survivors spoke of great flocks of birds circling overhead, even in the worst of the storms, as though the birds knew the doom to come. The survivors said they saw men on the beach, waving them on to their deaths. Ghosts of the *Rose,* beckoning the living onto the rocks. The bay's cursed, no doubt."

"Are you sure ghosts didn't tell you that story?" I chuckled, hoping to lighten the mood.

Martin spun away. "Laugh if you must, but that bay is damned."

I nodded, hoping to placate him. "So what do you know about the abbey?" I asked, changing the subject.

Martin stared at the painting of the sea bluff again. "It's at Winterbay, ain't it?"

"What?" I asked, not following him.

"*Everything* in that bay is cursed," he said.

I swallowed a bite of my burger. "Is that it? That's all you know about it?"

The bartender walked in front of Martin and wiped down the bar. He looked hard at the old man. "That's it," the bartender said. "The abbey's just an old building, there's no curse. I think a hotel is a great idea, perfect for the town."

"But all those kids—" Martin started, stopping as the bartender took a vicious swipe at a spot directly in front of him.

"Kids?" I asked. "What kids?"

They exchanged another glance. "Nothing," Martin grumbled as he swallowed his drink. "Just kids, playing games."

That was all Martin said the rest of the night. After the bartender brought his food, we ate silently, watching a late West Coast college football game on TV and awkwardly avoiding each other's looks.

I got up to leave. As I paid my tab and slid off my seat, Martin said, "Be careful when you're working up there. You don't want to get caught in one of the storms. One's coming. I can feel it."

I glanced at the TV. The five-day forecast scrolled along the bottom, a string of bright sunny graphics.

I waved at Martin, wishing him well, and left him to get a rise out of someone else. Martin's stories were fun, although I was glad I was an architect, not some lost fisherman trying to navigate the waters of Winterbay.

CHAPTER FOUR

At the end of the main thoroughfare, my windshield framed an old three-story Queen Anne sitting amidst a grove of leafless trees. Branches like gnarled fingers reached toward the upper levels of the inn, grasping it in large skeletal palms.

Charming.

The interior was not nearly as quaint nor historic as the outside. It had the sterile look of a 1980s redo, almost like a hospital, with bright fluorescent lights winking in the halls and thin carpet beneath sickly, beige-colored walls. A *Three Stooges* episode was running on a boxy TV attached to a side table.

I checked in and went up to my room on the top floor. I was looking forward to taking a hot shower and getting some sleep. I turned on the little gas fireplace and took in the fantastically gaudy furnishings. An ugly floral bedspread, attached wall hair dryer, and one-cup coffee maker gave it the standard look.

In the center of the small desk, a fat white vase trying to be Greek in style, but looking more oriental, held fake branches dotted with pussy willows. The perfect combination of uncombinable things. I chuckled at the large triptych painting of the *Niña*, the *Pinta*, and the *Santa Maria* hanging over the desk. After hearing Martin's stories, all I could see was them smashing on the rocks.

I threw my suitcase on the bed and unzipped it, looking for my pj bottoms and toothbrush. A wrapped gift lay between two pairs of jeans. A sudden sense of guilt overtook me, a sinking in my guts. Emily had been knitting something for a while, or trying to. A project, she said. The one she'd talked about selling online before I left.

A folded note lay atop a thick gray sweater:

> *Sorry for how things were left. Hope this cheers you up and thought you may need an extra layer to fight off that Maine chill.*
>
> *Love you so much,*
>
> *Emily*
>
> *P.S. Someone to look over you!*

She'd sketched a little angel, wings spread in flight.

I held up the sweater. Once upon a time, her creations were things of beauty, perfection. I fought back the temptation to look for mistakes, dropped stitches, hanging loops. *She tried so hard.* Surprisingly, the workmanship and fitted look reminded me of something you'd buy at an expensive European department store, just like her old ones. Maybe her hand was better than she let on.

Inside the back of the collar was a tiny embroidered heart. Hot pink stitching against the edges of red fiber formed an elegant contrast.

Except there it was, a dropped stitch near the tip of the heart. My stomach lurched.

Guilt at being too critical and weakness from missing her spread throughout my body in waves. I sat on the bed and clutched the sweater to my chest.

I grabbed my phone and tapped her name.

She picked up.

"Hey, it's me," I said.

"Hi. Did you make it to the hotel okay?" Emily asked, her voice edged with anxiety and also a little bit groggy.

"Yeah. Everything's fine. Did I wake you up?"

"Kinda," she said.

"Another nightmare?" I could almost see Emily rubbing her hand as she held the phone.

"Yeah. I guess I was taking a late nap. I just keep imagining losing the baby. It terrifies me. What if there is another accident?"

Did she mean what if there was *another* accident I couldn't save her from? Gut-punch.

She took a deep breath. "Sorry, everything seems to be getting to me more since…" she said, cutting off there. "Let's talk about something else. I'm glad you made it. I wish I was there, and I wanted to say sorry."

"It's okay. I'm sorry I had to leave you so quickly. Speaking of you being here…. I know this seems a little sudden, but would you want to come out here? Say, tomorrow?" The question left my mouth before I really even knew what I was asking.

"What? Are you *serious*? Wouldn't the plane ticket be expensive?"

I should have thought more about the cost. Except for some reason, the dread of being separated right now came on like a flood. "Just let me figure that part out." Maybe I could somehow make this another business expense. "I miss you. And I don't know why, but one week is just too long to be away right now. Are you fit to fly at four and a half months?"

She was silent for a second, but I could feel her smiling on the other end. She laughed just like she used to when we first met, making me long for old, carefree times.

"Yes, traveling is just fine now. Wow, maybe I should surprise you with a present every time you go away," she said playfully. "Did you get it?"

I laughed. "Yes, thank you for that! It looks amazing. I like your new embroidered heart. Where'd you find the design?"

"Thanks! That's the baby's symbol. I actually made it up myself. I'm going to put it on *everything* now," she said. "Important to stamp a piece of your personality onto whatever you're creating."

I inwardly groaned, thinking of the Greenwood Community Center.

"That must have taken a huge effort," I said. "I'm so proud of you."

"I accidentally skipped a stitch on the tip of the heart." Her voice dropped the way it did every time she talked about her hand.

"Don't worry. I'm not taking a microscope to your stitching," I said, lying and then feeling ashamed. "Hey, I hate to cut short, but I have to get going. Long day ahead, and I'm going to grab your ticket online right now. I'll email the details."

"Okay! I'm so happy," she said.

"Love you, and I'll see you tomorrow," I said.

I put my phone down. Maybe a change of scenery would help both of us. My mind swam with images of Emily smiling and laughing like when we met in college. I wanted her to be happy like that again.

I expected the looming loneliness of missing Emily to go away. Instead, it intensified. Trying to shrug it off, I jumped onto the web to buy the ticket.

After I finished, I got into the shower and then bed. The knot in my stomach morphed into a cold stone. I turned over and hoped that whatever was ailing me would be gone by morning.

I slept restlessly, unable to get comfortable. Someone's baby cried off and on. What little sleep I got was plagued by strange nightmares. Weird black shapes stalked me and sprung out from dark corners of an endless labyrinth. I never had bad dreams. I must have been tossing and turning because the comforter was on the floor when I woke up.

A faint moonlit glow bathed the room. I glanced over at the clock. 3:07. I still had the knot in my stomach, and my neck ached from a lumpy pillow.

I groggily made my way to the bathroom and drank some water as I stared into the mirror. Blankly, I rubbed my eyes. Dark circles contrasted with my pale skin. I looked like hell.

A reflected flash outside the window caught my eye.

I quickly turned around, and my breath caught in my throat. A distorted face peered through the glass.

I looked closer. It was a woman, her face masked by wild, wind-swept hair. Fearful, I hurried over to the window. The face began to distort. The lines reformed, twisting, intertwining, taking on a geometric shape. When I reached the window, I recognized the Grecian vase reflected in the glass.

I sat down on the side of the bed and held my head.

Okay, I really needed to try to relax.

I glanced over at the window again; it still twisted the vase's reflection. I got up, closed the curtains, and put the vase under the desk. It was an eyesore anyway.

Back in bed, I closed my eyes and listened to the tick of the clock.

CHAPTER FIVE

Morning came too soon. I zombied my way to the bathroom, noticing my wild hair.

Groggily, I got ready, put on my new sweater, and headed to the car.

The weather was sunny but cold. Really cold. The kind of surprising November chill that makes your fingers turn blue in a matter of minutes. I was glad for the sweater's extra warmth.

As I closed the car door, I had an overwhelming urge to go back into my room, lock myself in, and sleep the whole day.

I put my palm to my forehead. My skin felt warm, but my fingers were freezing.

I pressed the start button on the car. The female voice said to head three miles past my hotel, then turn right and go four miles on Old Quarry road to the turn off to the abbey.

The main route cut through heavy forest filled with deciduous trees we don't see much of in Washington. I wished I could have been here a month earlier to see the bright oranges and yellows before the leaves fell. Now the brown, dead remnants of the kaleidoscope of autumn foliage swirled across the road in a breezy parade of lost beauty.

Two miles from the abbey turn off, according to the GPS, I got stuck behind a couple of dump trucks. They turned off onto a side driveway choked with mud from the layer of wet snow. I almost had a heart attack when I swerved to avoid a third that pulled in front of me from the same driveway. That's all I needed, crushed by a two-ton truck on my first day.

I stuck my hand up to flip off the jerk, then remembered I was from Seattle and we're too polite to do that. The gravel-filled truck told me the road name was accurate. I hoped for the developers' sake that the quarry wasn't blasting. Explosions never make for a good vacation experience.

I continued past the quarry until I reached a barely legible, rotted sign for Winterbay Abbey. I stopped and looked down the side road that headed toward the water. The bright morning sun glinted through the bare trees and illuminated a curving gravel driveway. The snow was mostly melted, leaving only a mushy layer of slush.

This is really out of the way.

Snow sloshed under my tires as I drove the last mile toward the abbey. A mother deer and two fawns pranced across the road. They stopped to stare at the car.

I slowed.

The mother almost seemed to motion me to follow as she hopped into the tree cover. Cute as they were, the animals only increased my sense of isolation. When I'd first examined the plans, the property sounded like the perfect setting, a wild and magnificent location for a five-star hotel. Now that I was here, the idea of being isolated from civilization pressed on me.

The file mentioned Winterbay Abbey had been closed since the late 1960s. The nuns who ran it grew old and no new ones replaced them.

The closer I got to the water, the less snow there was until it disappeared altogether. Rounding a particularly sharp curve, I crossed a small wooden bridge and finally reached the abbey's grounds. The plans I'd read said there were twenty acres of open parkland around the main building, which itself sat on a rocky bluff overlooking the shore.

The grounds were as large as advertised, but having been abandoned for nearly forty years, the property had taken on much the same densely wooded look as the surrounding forest.

I drove through an overarching rusted iron gate toward the main entry.

The abbey loomed in front of me on a low rocky outcrop with its back braced against the sea. Three stories of faded, weather-worn red brick, aged and decrepit but still noble, stood above a broad stairway leading to the front entrance and large archway that bisected the building. Moss and the emaciated remains of ivy covered much of the brickwork.

Gray slate tiles, some having slid away and broken on the cracked sidewalk beneath, topped the gabled roof. The transom windows had spidered and broken. The paint had long ago peeled away from the frames and sashes.

One wing on the south connected to the main building, forming an L facing the sea. A large bell tower, looking even more worn than the photos Lance had given me, stood above the wing on its far end, closest to and overlooking the water. I stopped when I saw the tower, half-expecting that mesmerizing feeling from the photo to return. But now it was just an architectural element.

I always looked for the best in any project, and what others thought of as "brooding," I liked to call "charm." The abbey's bones reminded me of Emily's old dorm from our alma mater, the University of Washington. At least that's how I wanted to see it. I spent a lot of time in that dorm, once in a while noticing its architectural features when Emily wasn't capturing all my attention.

I walked up the steps, several split and crumbling, to the main archway. It led back to an open courtyard. I imagined this space inside the L as outdoor seating for a fine restaurant with a spectacular view, although in its current state it more closely resembled a graveyard of broken stones. I could see the waves crashing below on the rocky beach at the bottom of the short cliff not more than thirty yards from the building. Beyond that loomed the cold bay—the cursed bay of "lost souls" as Martin had called it—and then the might of the North Atlantic.

This area truly had the most beautiful and rugged scenery I'd ever seen, in many ways similar to—but even more striking than—the Pacific Northwest coast. As I scanned the horizon, a spike of red caught my eye. The tall lighthouse Martin spoke of stood about a quarter mile offshore on its own rock. It reminded me of an abandoned lighthouse off Cannon Beach in Oregon, now home to seabirds. It was a tall, tapering spire with a glass lantern room at the top covered by a fading red roof. A thick, navy-blue swirl cascaded down its thin white body. Waves broke over its rocky base and splashed up the sides.

Another sight caught my eye, this one more dismal. Set back about fifty yards from the shore, just inside the tree line, was a tangle of gray headstones. I shivered. I hadn't expected a cemetery. This was more than likely the abbey's graveyard, and its Gothic style further enhanced the property's old-world look. Still, for a hotel…I tried not to think about what might be necessary to do with what guests would see as a chilling eyesore.

Apart from the graveyard, it was easy to see why the developers had snatched this property. The only wonder was why it had sat empty for so long. After some serious renovation, it would scream money.

I glanced toward the abbey's main doors. I had to get to work. I'd need to do a thorough inspection of the building's general condition. Mechanical and structural engineers generally did more careful poking around. But I liked to get my hands dirty and not leave them with the task of fitting everything into fairy-tale drawings, which I knew they hated.

A cold blast of wind almost froze me to the ground as I hunched my shoulders and headed inside.

A grand staircase with stone steps stood just inside the main entry. It made for a magnificent first impression upon entering. The front door hung ajar, held in place by a single hinge. I shook my head. The longer the building had been open to the elements, the more it would cost to refurbish—if it could be done at all. I feared what I might find further inside. Many old, abandoned institutional buildings became frightening haunts of decay and rot.

I peeked past the door. Sunlight streamed in, enough to illuminate piles of rubbish littering the front hall. Despite being out in the woods miles from town, people clearly had been here. I hoped they weren't still here. One pile had been used for a fire, and recently.

On one wall was scrawled, *P, I love you; forgive me,* in barely faded bright red paint. A red heart encased the *P*.

Some homeless guy had no doubt left his plea. "Hello!" I called. "Is anyone there?"

Dealing with squatters was part of the job, but not a part I'd ever enjoyed. Back in Seattle, I'd been threatened with a knife just walking around Belltown. I didn't want any repeats.

A faraway crack split the air, echoing through the woods and off the building.

Blasting at the quarry. *Wonderful.*

I called out again. "Hello?"

No answer. First squatters and now explosions. I swallowed and stepped inside, wishing I was alone. Something skittered down the dark hall.

"Hello!"

I grabbed a flashlight from my pocket and shined the beam down the corridor. Dust like a million stars danced in the light. Something creaked above my head. I jerked the light to the ceiling, but there was nothing except more dust and a forest of spider webs. I thought of Martin's stories of Winterbay and its ghosts. I took a deep breath to calm my nerves. *Get a grip.*

Whoever had been here was gone, I told myself. A rat was probably scurrying around.

That wasn't much better. I was sure the place was filled with pests. Driving out rats was one of the most difficult things about a complete renovation of a long-empty site. The vermin don't like to leave, and they're harder to eradicate than a whiny love song stuck in your head. Luckily, I just drew the plans. Someone else cleaned out the rats.

"I'm coming in!" I called, hoping if a homeless guy did still live here he'd avoid me. I wandered through the main floor and then went upstairs, weaving my way past curtains of cobwebs hung over doorways. The smell was pungent, almost suffocating. The dust had a sour odor that went beyond the normal aroma of neglected buildings.

For the most part, the squatters seemed to have stuck to the ground floor. The second floor was filled with dorm rooms, or cells as they called them in abbeys or monasteries, by and large empty except for old iron beds with thin mattresses, stiff wooden chairs, and tiny desks. All in all, there was less degradation than I'd feared. The elements had largely been kept out.

I went up to the third floor.

A lump of black bunched up against the wall made me do a double take. It lay outside the door of a room where the hall turned at the L toward the bell tower. I shined my flashlight on it. It looked like a pile of clothes.

I picked up the bundle and dust cascaded off the folds. The material reminded me of cloth used for drapes, stiff and heavy. I sneezed and held it in front of me, revealing what looked like a black skirt and square-cut top—something like a nun's outfit, a habit. I turned my light back down the hall. No footprints other than mine in the thick dust. It must have been a long time since anyone had been up here. Had a nun really left this here years ago? It seemed strange that it would have been discarded like this. Despite the covering of dust, the material was in pretty good shape for something decades old.

As I turned down the south wing, the sunlight dimmed, and a dampness in the air made the space noticeably cooler. Just as on the second floor, all the doors here were closed, shutting out the natural light. I tried the doorknob on the room at the end of the hall. From the position of the door, the room appeared to be larger than the others. It was locked.

I tested the key Lance had left in the file. The knob wiggled but wouldn't open. I shook it harder. It remained firmly shut.

The room next door was unlocked, so I opened it to let in some light to inspect the knob on the locked door. I tried it again. This time the knob turned easily. Weird. Maybe it had been stuck before, and my wiggling had loosened it. I pushed it open with a slow creak.

I'd been right. This room was larger than the others and seemed more communal. The furniture inside was the same iron-framed beds with mattresses, lined up in rows of six, with rickety chairs stacked on top of desks shoved into the far corner. Perhaps the novitiates had slept here, keeping them together.

I used my laser tape to gather the dimensions, thinking about where to put a bathroom and hot tub for a suite. Backing away from one wall to get a better look, I banged into one of the beds, stumbled and cracked my shin on another bed frame.

"Sonofabitch!" I cried out and leaned over to rub my leg. I shook my head, cursing the pain away as I balanced against a frame. As I held my shin, I noticed a small knitted blanket on the bed. It was sky blue and looked handmade. Something about it looked familiar. I leaned closer, and my eyes locked on the top right corner. Close to the edge, an embroidered red heart was sewn in with pink stitching.

I picked it up and shook off the dust. It was tiny, something knit for an infant. The look was almost identical to what Emily had sewn into my sweater. Hadn't she said she made up this design herself? And recently? Yet its discoloration was identical to the mattress. It had been here for decades.

I pulled off my jacket and sweater. Cold weather or not, I needed to make sure I wasn't losing my mind. I shivered as I held up my embroidered heart next to the one on the blanket. They were identical, same shape and color, and the blankets had even been stitched in the same proportions. I looked closer, and my mouth dropped. A missed stitch at the tip of the heart.

I swallowed. My heart pounded in my ears.

Maybe Emily had copied a pattern, perhaps a style popular years ago. But her hand…she said she'd made a mistake with the stitching.

How could the same error be on this blanket, in the same spot?

After putting my sweater and jacket back on, I rolled up the blanket and tucked it under my arm.

It could be just a weird coincidence, but I needed to show this to Emily.

CHAPTER SIX

I put the blanket in the car for safekeeping, glad to be rid of it, but the whole embroidered heart stitching was too bizarre to ignore. While I tried to stay focused on my work the rest of the morning, the image of that heart clung to my thoughts. I hesitated at every door, wondering what new strangeness I might find.

I resisted the temptation to leave early and split my pre-design work into two days. I needed to get the entire lay of the land for my meeting with the developers the next day.

I headed to the courtyard after grabbing my pad and Lamy pen to get some sketches of the outside of the building with the shoreline in both the fore- and background. For the most part, I drew up my plans on the computer, but I always did hand sketches to brainstorm ideas for remodels. Thoughts on paper were also convenient to run by Emily, who had an artist's eye and more taste than I'd ever developed.

My breath made white puffs as I walked through the archway into the courtyard. Flying low overhead, a flock of birds squawked. The wind had died down, and I could make out the sound of their wings beating in unison. I rubbed my arms for warmth as a wider angle of the lighthouse and beach came into view. From the hotel to the beach—which was mostly rough, broken rock and tide pools—was a tall grassy area populated with a few wind-blown, scrawny pines. The beach itself was fine for viewing, but little else. A chill mist sat out on the bay, and waves crashed onto the rocks, spraying a large sign:

DANGEROUS CURRENTS
NO SWIMMING

It seemed odd that anyone would even think of going into those cold, violent waters for a swim. Then again everything today seemed to have some sort of warning to keep lawyers at bay.

I flipped open my notepad and began sketching the old building as a summer wonderland, a hotel that would have been at home in Newport, Rhode Island or the Jersey shore of 1890, complete with women in bustles holding parasols and men with straw hats and striped jackets.

Off to my left, a movement on the beach caught my eye. A thin figure stood on the grass, close to where the turf transitioned into rock, 150 yards or so distant. I waited for it to move. It stood still. I added a few lines. I flipped the page, wondering who else could be out here. Was my squatter out enjoying the view, or perhaps waiting for me to leave so he could reoccupy his dilapidated home?

I squinted into the sun and wandered down toward the beach to have a better look.

The figure remained, unmoving. I walked closer. It turned. I saw a face, a skirt blowing in the wind. My companion was a girl in her early twenties, if that. A black skirt hung below her knees, and a white-fringed headpiece caught the wind. A nun's habit. Was she visiting the abbey? There was no car in the lot except mine.

I waved and made my way toward her, glad of some small company in this lonely place. My worry about confronting a knife-wielding vagrant vanished. It would also be interesting to see if she had any information regarding the abbey's history. She remained still, unmoving. *I guess she hadn't seen me.* Maybe her eyes were closed in prayer. I stopped and waited, maybe seventy yards away, not wanting to interrupt. It was freezing out here, though. The girl stood stone-stiff in the breeze. I shivered from the cold and then realized she didn't have a jacket. She had to be frozen.

Her head tipped back. She smiled at me, but in a vacant way, as if she'd looked through me to something beyond.

Then her look changed. My heart pounded suddenly, dread winding through my chest. Something about the nun's face set off alarm bells. Her smile. Cold, angry, frightened, hateful—a prism of emotions spewed out from her grin and assaulted me from that one look. I stumbled and fell into the tall grass as though physically struck, the force of her eyes so powerful.

The crashing of the waves rang in my ears. I heard the sound of a motor coming from offshore, then a ruffling, like the beat of wings. I glanced toward the sea. There was no sign of any boat, and the earlier flock of birds had gone. I closed my eyes and willed my heart to slow its racing. What was wrong with me? *Get a hold of yourself.*

I took a deep breath and wobbled to my feet. The hum of the motorboat sounded closer. I scanned the water. Nothing except whitecaps.

My head felt fuzzy, and I nearly fell again. When I looked down the beach, I spotted the girl walking slowly over the wave-splashed rocks toward the water, her arms outstretched above her, head tilted back.

I glanced upward, following her gaze. A large flock of seagulls soared by. She stared at them. A moment later, the birds vanished behind a forested hillside. Then she stepped into the surf.

What the hell was she *doing*? The water was ice-cold. She walked steadily forward without lifting her feet, sure-footed in the surf and slippery rocks. I watched as the water came up over her hips.

"Hey!" I cried, waving.

She did not look back at me. I was oddly grateful, yet ashamed, for not wanting to see that face again. The water rose to her shoulders.

"Hey!" I repeated, racing toward her. She neither flinched nor turned away from the pounding waves.

I sprinted down the beach, calling all the way. "Come back! It's not safe!" She didn't respond. Without thinking, I raced into the surf, slipping on one of the rocks and tumbling headfirst into the waves. The intense cold took my breath away. The waves forced me under. A sharp pain gouged my forehead as my head hit a jagged rock.

My head aching and spinning, I pushed myself above the cresting water. Gasping for breath, I looked for the girl. A wave rolled in and pushed me onto my back. I coughed and choked, spitting out salt water. The nun was nowhere in sight.

I scrambled back ashore to get a better look, hoping she'd come to her senses and retreated from the waves onto the beach. Still no sign of anyone on land or in the ocean. I glanced around again for a boat. The noise of the motor had stopped.

Shaking and chilled to my core, I reached into my pocket for my phone. My head pounded from my encounter with the rock, and blood dripped down into my eyes. A concussion? I had to call 911. I'd never felt this cold in my entire life. The girl wouldn't last long out in the water.

I looked for my phone.

All my pockets were empty.

"Damn it!"

I scanned the rocky beach. Where was my phone? I searched the large stones, not seeing the stupid thing anywhere.

There was no point in looking for it any longer. I had to get help. I raced back to my car. Carelessly, I drove back to the main road, speeding down the narrow winding turns.

CHAPTER SEVEN

I was still shaking violently when I got back to the hotel. I crashed through the doors to get to the front desk and use the phone. The dispatcher said she would send a rescue squad and inform the Coast Guard. She asked if I was okay. I looked at my hands. My fingertips had a slight bluish tinge. I still had a headache but wasn't seeing double or anything, and the blood was a dried smear on my face. An emergency room visit was not something I wanted. I was actually thankful Emily wasn't here. She would have made me go. I'd probably be fine after a hot shower, a warm drink, and some rest.

"Yes, I'm okay. Thanks," I said.

"Okay, the water rescue squad will be there soon," she said. "Please stay on the phone until the first responders arrive."

"I'm not at the scene," I told her. "I lost my phone and had to find a place to call. I'm at the Blackwoods Hotel."

The dispatcher was silent for a moment, then said, "Okay. We'll send an officer to speak with you." She hung up.

The clerk looked me up and down. A weary expression crossed her face.

"I'll send the police up to your room when they arrive," she said, shuffling papers.

"Thanks for your help and for—"

She shook her head and turned away, ignoring me.

"Is something wrong?" I asked.

She turned back with a sigh. "Aren't you a little old for this? Halloween is over."

"What's that supposed to mean?" I asked.

She rolled her eyes. "Most people know when to give up." She reached under the counter and pulled out a first-aid kit. "That head wound is taking it a bit far. Get yourself cleaned up."

The phone rang before I could ask her again what the hell she was talking about. She turned away and picked it up. "Blackwoods Hotel. The 20th? Yes, we have a vacancy then."

Taking my cue, I left. I'd had enough for today. But I wondered what sort of small-town insider knowledge I was missing. Martin had mentioned something about kids up at the abbey.

I walked upstairs, rubbing my head. The clerk was right about one thing. I must have looked like walking death.

I got to my room, turned up the heat, and jumped in the shower. The hot water made my skin tingle. As water streamed down my face, I replayed the scene from the beach, and my stomach began to ache. I sank to the floor, overcome by the certainty I was too late calling the police, and the nun had drowned.

About five minutes after I dried off and changed, there was a knock. I opened the door to a man in his mid-forties wearing a blue police uniform.

"Will Larson?"

"Yes," I said, opening the door wider.

The officer stepped in. "Officer Vaughn. Did you report a drowning?"

"Yes," I said. "Out at Winterbay Abbey. Have you found the girl?"

"We've got officers and an ambulance at Winterbay Abbey now, and the Search and Rescue Squad has a boat out." He glared directly into my eyes. "I take it you're not from around here."

"No," I said. "I'm from Seattle. I'm here to design a renovation for the abbey."

Vaughn nodded. "You've got a wound on your head. Have you had it looked at?"

I winced as I brushed the gash on my forehead. "It's not as bad as it looks."

"Well, you don't look too good," he said. "When's the last time you got any sleep? It's a long flight from Seattle."

"Um, last night," I said. "Look, you didn't come here to ask about my health."

"No," he said, reaching into a jacket pocket for a pad and pen. "Why don't you recount what you saw."

I told him the story, the woman, even the strange detail about hearing the boat and the sound of flapping wings.

The officer's face remained expressionless. I couldn't help but notice the broken violet capillaries under his eyes and the red spider veins that webbed across his face. *I guess being a cop was hard everywhere.*

"I think she was a nun," I said.

"Nun?" He stopped and glanced up from his notes. "Why do you say that?"

"The way she dressed. Habits, I think they're called."

He tapped his pen on his notepad. "You know how kids dress these days," he said. "My own daughter only wears black. It's that whole goth, emo thing, whatever they call it."

"I know what I saw. There was nothing fashionable about her clothes."

"That's what I tell my daughter every day."

"Are there nuns in the area?" I asked.

"No," Officer Vaughn said.

"Not any?"

"No."

"Well, that was an abbey. Maybe nuns go there sometimes to—"

He shook his head. "That place has been abandoned for years. The nuns were all transferred away long ago. You couldn't have seen a nun."

"That seems odd. Why not?"

"They're all gone." He tapped a button on his phone. I recognized the distinctive beep. He'd recorded this entire conversation. I thought police were supposed to ask permission before they did that.

"Okay, fine," I said. "But I did see a woman down there. And I found a nun's habit inside the abbey."

Vaughn stopped for a moment. "Inside?"

"Yes."

He took a deep breath and muttered, "Damned kids." Then to me, "Well, we're looking, as I said."

"Kids?" I asked. "Were there some kids out at the abbey or something?"

"I still have more questions for you," he said, cutting me off.

I guess I wasn't going to get any small-town insider information today.

"Wait, can you at least tell me if you've found a body?" I asked.

He shook his head. "We'll keep at it. If no one is reported missing by tomorrow or the next day…" he trailed off.

"Then what?" I asked.

"You're sure it was a girl?" he asked again, still tapping his pen. "You may have seen a sign, or a tree on the beach."

"Signs or trees don't walk into the water."

"Why did you leave the scene?" he asked.

"My cell phone washed away, and I needed to find a phone so I could call the paramedics."

Just then my hotel phone rang. "Excuse me one moment," I said. I picked up the receiver.

"Is this Will Larson?" a man asked on the other end.

"Yes." I didn't recognize the voice.

"This is Ted Alderstone. I'm out at Winterbay Abbey."

"Oh, yeah, hey," I said.

"There's an ambulance out here, the Coast Guard is searching the bay, and the door to the abbey is wide open. We've been trying to track you down. James and I came out today because we knew you were going to be here. Do you want to tell me what is going on at our property?" he asked with an edge to his tone.

Crap. I scratched the back of my neck, feeling a little warm all of the sudden. "Um, there was an accident."

The cop gave me a quizzical look. I wished he'd shown himself the door already. I didn't appreciate the third degree.

"Well, we figured that much," Ted said.

"Yeah, hey, I'm actually with the police right now. Can I call you back?" I asked.

"You're with the *police*?" Ted asked.

"Yeah, they needed to ask me a few questions. There was a drowning out in the bay. I can fill you in on the rest soon," I said.

He went silent.

"Hello?" I asked.

"We're still expecting to meet with you tomorrow to look over the preliminary ideas and get this all sorted out," he said.

Damn it.

I'd left my drawings on the beach, and I was sure, like my cell phone, they were now long gone. It would take the rest of the day, with time to pick up Emily at the airport, and another night of no sleep to work up some conceptual sketches.

"Yes, of course," I said. "I'll be there bright and early." The phone clicked.

"Mr. Larson, I'd like you to come back with me to the abbey. Maybe we can get some better details there and guide the rescue workers," Vaughn said.

So much for getting started on those plans. "Of course. Do you have any idea when we might be back here?" I needed all the time I could get, although I felt like a bit of a jerk for asking.

A blast of static and a voice from the officer's radio interrupted me. He picked up his radio. "On my way," he said and quickly clipped it back to his belt. "Not sure how long. Come on," he said. "Let's go."

CHAPTER EIGHT

The ride to Winterbay Abbey in the back of a police car was like a night in jail. The bulletproof glass dividing the front and back seats conjured a prison vibe. I wondered what kinds of small-town criminals actually had sat back here.

I wanted to make small talk, but Officer Vaughn kept asking me questions I'd already answered at the hotel. So much so that I started to wonder if I needed to hire a lawyer. He didn't think I was making this up, did he?

We rounded the particularly sharp curve I remembered from earlier this morning and drove across the small wooden bridge. After passing a grove of pines, we came upon the old abbey's grounds. Winterbay Abbey dominated the landscape.

Red lights flashed in front of the main entrance. I counted one ambulance, two police cars, and a water rescue truck. No sign of Ted or James' car, whatever that might be. They must have already left, not knowing I was coming back. In some ways, I wished they hadn't.

"They're waiting on us," Officer Vaughn said. He pulled into the parking lot and thankfully let me out. I shivered as he shut the car door, wishing I had an extra jacket.

Two men in the ambulance had their windows down with the heater running full blast.

"Anything?" Officer Vaughn asked.

"Nothing. Search and Rescue is still out, though," the driver said. He stopped and looked at me. "Is this the guy?"

Vaughn nodded. "That's him."

"I thought Halloween was over," the driver said, echoing the hotel clerk.

Vaughn shook his head.

They both looked at me while I tried to figure out what they meant.

"Nobody saw Duncan, did they?" Vaughn asked.

"Not that I know of," the paramedic said. "That would have made my day."

"Mr. Larson, would you mind coming with me, please?" Vaughn asked, hands on his hips like I was the one who had been making him wait.

"Hey, hold on. What did he mean about Halloween?" I asked. "The clerk at the hotel said something similar."

"Childish pranks," Vaughn said. "Same thing every year. On Halloween, we get the typical kids egging and toilet-papering houses, like everywhere. But we also get girls coming out here. They dress up as nuns to scare each other and make a nuisance. The history of this place, or legends anyway, are somewhat of a local tradition."

This must have been what Martin was alluding to.

"Not very funny if you ask me. But it may explain the nun's habit you saw inside the abbey. And in all honesty, that 'drowning' you witnessed could've just been some girl dressed up as a prank," Vaughn said.

"That was no prank. And there is no way I'd fly from Seattle to play a joke."

Vaughn stopped and spun on me. "I don't think you played a prank, no. But you may have been fooled by one."

"I don't see it," I said. "I'm not that gullible."

"Well, we'll see. I haven't made up my mind about anything. Let's take a look at the beach and see if you can add any details to your story."

Great. Now I knew why I was getting the runaround. Apparently I was either a liar or a fool.

No one believed a girl had actually died.

We walked up through the archway and into the courtyard. I heard the sound of a motor out in the water again, very much like the earlier one. Except this came from a big boat marked Berkeley County Search and Rescue. Besides the larger boat, two men in cold-water diving suits slowly drove their inflatable raft along the shore, looking closely at the sea. I spotted two other men dressed like Vaughn in the distance, walking the beach.

"This is where I first saw the girl." I tried to focus, thinking twice about each word I said. I wanted to make sure my true story didn't sound made up.

Vaughn stared at me.

"I spotted her down there, on the grass." I pointed off to the south.

"How far?"

"About 150 yards, maybe a little more," I said.

Vaughn scratched his stubbled chin. "How much could you see from that distance?"

"Not much," I admitted. "That's why I ran down there to get closer."

"Why were you so eager to chase down a girl on the beach?" he asked.

I shook my head, my jaw clenching. "What's that supposed to mean?" I asked.

"Just answer the question," Vaughn said, glaring at me. "Why did you run after her?"

I took a quick glance down the beach. The two divers hauled their raft up onto the rocks.

"I didn't run at first," I told him. "I saw she was a nun, and I thought maybe she could tell me about the abbey, about its history." I left out the freak anxiety attack I had when the girl looked at me. Vaughn already distrusted me. No need to make him question my sanity.

"There are no nuns here," Vaughn said.

"Yeah, so you keep telling me," I said. "There *was* a girl on the beach, dressed like a nun, costume or not. I don't know where she came from. And I saw her wade out into the ocean and not come back. I don't appreciate being called a liar."

Vaughn waved his hands. "Calm down," he said. "No one's calling you a liar. It's just that parts of your story don't make a lot of sense." He turned and nodded to the divers, who had walked up behind him. They both shook their heads. Vaughn looked back at me. "Like the fact there was no other car when we first got here. Did you see another car? If the girl had drowned she couldn't have driven it anywhere, and this place is pretty isolated. It's a long, cold hike on foot without a car."

I shook my head. "I didn't see any cars. But I did hear a boat. Maybe she was dropped off on shore."

Vaughn scratched his chin. "Or picked up. My prank theory could explain that. She had friends, and they drove off in a car, or boat, when you weren't looking."

"But why play a prank on me? What sense does that make? I'm from out of town, no one knows me. Was my itinerary circulated at the high school?"

Vaughn shrugged. "Kids come out here to play jokes. You showed up, and they played one on you. You see what we're dealing with here, don't you? There's really no indication of anyone besides you being out here."

"I don't know about everything else, but it's a big ocean." I pointed to the sign on the beach. "And obviously this is a dangerous spot, with treacherous currents and an undertow. Why would someone drowning be so unbelievable?"

"Do you know how cold that water is?" Vaughn asked.

A chill went through my whole body, remembering how icy the surf was. "Yeah, I was in it. Look, is it my job to explain the mental state of people I see drowning before I report it? I didn't have time to run a psychological analysis to find out if her motivations were believable, or check on her transportation options."

"All right," Vaughn said. "But you see my point. I'm just trying to work through this as best I can. You didn't actually see the girl drown?"

I nodded. "I slipped on the rocks and fell in the water. When I came up she was gone."

One of the divers spoke up. "Not seeing anything," he said to Vaughn. Looking at me he added, "I've done a lot of searches in these waters. With waves like this, it's hard to see anyone. The girl may have been out there, and you'd never be able to spot her. A human head is no bigger than a volleyball. And unlike a ball it doesn't float."

Vaughn nodded and looked back at me. "Or more likely when you were in the water, or even after you ran for help, the girl came out and you missed her."

The image of the nun's face, the stabbing glare that seemed to reach in and pull on something, my soul, flashed through my mind. "I don't think she wanted to get out," I said.

Vaughn stopped and stared at me. "What do you mean?"

"I think she may have drowned herself on purpose," I said.

"Suicide?" Vaughn asked. He swallowed and glanced at the divers. "What makes you think that? I thought you weren't doing psychoanalysis."

I sighed. "As you say, the water is too cold for swimming. And the girl walked straight in, no hesitation."

Vaughn cleared his throat. "Well, the coroner would have to make that determination, and we'd need a body for that."

The diver glanced at Vaughn. "We'll go back out in a bit, and the Coast Guard will keep searching further out."

"Thanks, Nick," Vaughn said, patting him on the shoulder. "I'll walk up the beach to see if we missed her washing ashore. If she got swept out, she could show up anywhere in the bay."

Vaughn lowered his voice, but I still managed to catch the end of what he said. "Stupid kids….I'm sure nothing will turn up."

The diver nodded and glanced at me. "Let's hope."

Vaughn coughed into his fist. "Yeah. Glad Duncan didn't show up."

From what they said I could tell they still thought I had been the butt of a joke. And who was this Duncan they kept mentioning?

Vaughn looked back at me. "I guess that's all we need, for now. I have your number at the hotel. Ask the ambulance driver for a ride. We'll be in touch."

Vaughn walked off down the beach, and both divers made their way back to the water. I was thankful no one had asked me to help search for a body.

As I wandered back to the abbey, I began to question just what I had seen. Could Vaughn be right? Could I have fallen for some teenage post-Halloween prank? Apparently it was a well-practiced ritual around here. Still, I'd gotten very lucky—or unlucky—just wandering by while it was happening. It couldn't have been planned on my behalf.

I shook my head. Then I remembered my sketchpad. I didn't want to have to redo all my work for the meeting with Ted and James tomorrow if I didn't have to. I'd dropped the pad somewhere in the grass. Maybe it was still here. I started retracing my steps, laying down my best guess for the path I'd taken from the courtyard to the water.

I spotted the book right away, lying open, the pages bent and damp with sea air. Thank God. I picked it up and flipped to the last sheet I'd been working on to see how well it had survived. It was the restoration drawing of a late-19th-century resort populated by well-to-do vacationers. I'd penned a detailed outline of the building and even a few couples strolling along the beach and sipping drinks in the courtyard restaurant. The page had been bent at one corner.

I stared at the picture. The elegant resort was no longer there. Instead, the drawing depicted the abbey as it stood now. Decrepit. Old. Each thin ink mark was defined, oddly focusing the entire sketch. Sharp, violent hatch marks scaled the shadowed areas all over the page and on the front of the bell tower was an oculus window.

My mouth went dry.

I had not drawn this.

I flipped through the pages. All my other drawings were there, just as I remembered them. Front view, courtyard, lighthouse.

I felt my head. Did I have a concussion? I held up my index and middle finger and saw only two digits.

My skin prickled, and I felt like I was suddenly being watched. I whipped around and scanned the beach. No one was in sight except for Vaughn down the beach, speaking with the two other officers.

A headache at the base of my skull added to the pain from my forehead. I squeezed my eyes shut for a moment to deaden the pain. Then I turned and dashed back toward the abbey with my sketchbook in hand.

Another blast from the quarry echoed through the trees.

I looked up at the bell tower on the way to the parking lot. No sign of the circular window in the sketch. I jumped when one of the paramedics yelled to me.

"Hey, buddy! Do you want a ride back into town?" He waved. "Vaughn just gave us the go-ahead to leave. Comin'?"

I tucked my sketchbook underneath my jacket. It was all I could do to not break out into a sprint.

CHAPTER NINE

It was 9:00 PM when Emily's plane finally landed. I'd fallen asleep on one of the rows of connected chairs. When she woke me, I grabbed her and wrapped my arms around her, almost afraid to let go.

She stepped back and looked at me. A flash of worry wrinkled her brow as she inspected my face. "Whoa, are you okay? I got your message. You lost your phone?" She leaned back and looked at me. "What happened to your head?" She softly brushed the bandage I'd put on my wound.

I hadn't told Emily the whole story in my message, especially about going into the water. I didn't want her worrying. "Let's get going," I said. "I'll explain in the car."

She put her hand on my arm. "Will, you're scared. I've never seen you like this," she said.

"I'm fine, just not sleeping much. You know, jet lag. And maybe with the baby coming I've been a little bit more on edge. I'll get through it."

Emily looked down at her feet. She only did that when something was wrong.

"What's that look?" I asked.

"Nothing, everything's fine," she said, still not meeting my eyes.

I stood there for a moment waiting for her to say something. She didn't.

I didn't have the strength to pull an answer out of her. "The car's this way," I said a little sheepishly.

As soon as we got in the rental, I blasted the heater, knowing she loved the warmth.

"You said on the message that a nun maybe drowned. I thought Winterbay Abbey was abandoned," Emily said.

"It is…I just…I still don't know what to make of all of this. The police said they'd give me a call when they knew something."

"That sounds so horrible. I'm so sorry you had to go through that." She reached out and squeezed my hand.

"It's all so strange, and it isn't the only bizarre thing that happened today."

"Oh?" she asked.

"Could you do me a favor? Take a look in the glove compartment."

She took out the tiny knit blanket I'd found in the abbey. "Gross, what is this? It smells awful. Did someone bury a cat in it?" she asked with a laugh.

A nervous chuckle escaped my lips. "Open it and look at the top right corner," I said.

"But it's beyond dirty and…"

I glanced over quickly. Emily was staring at the blanket, her mouth agape. "Where the hell did you get this?"

"Inside the abbey. Did you copy your symbol from some old pattern book or something?"

"No, I just made it up on the fly. I don't understand. Even the mistake I made with the stitching is here. Is this some kind of weird joke? Because it isn't funny, Will."

"No, it's not a joke. It's nothing. Probably just a coincidence. Someone just lost a baby blanket. Don't worry about it."

Emily stuffed the blanket back in the glove box. I waited for her to say something because I was at a loss to say anything comforting at this point. She just sat back in her seat.

The rest of the drive to the hotel was silent, just like to the airport yesterday.

I should have just asked her if she had copied the pattern from somewhere without showing her the blanket. *Idiot.* Now that I knew Emily hadn't duplicated the pattern, my vague fears deepened. I tried to tell myself it was just a simple heart. I wasn't convinced.

We pulled into the hotel parking lot. The same boney branches reached toward the inn, a stark contrast against the bright moon.

Emily glanced up. "Charming."

"It's not so bad. It's actually quite nice inside." I bit my lip, thinking I'd regret that fib later.

We made our way to our room. I put Emily's bags down, and she hung up her coat. She put her hand on the small of her back and sighed.

"Too long in an airplane seat?" I asked.

She nodded. "The guy next to me kept his seat tray down so he could nurse his cup of water for three hours. You don't know what it's like to hold it until you've had a baby sitting on your bladder."

"I don't want to find out," I said. "Hey, how about a fire?" A little heat sounded nice and cozy right now, and I needed something to get my mind off the "nun" at the beach and the blanket.

"Sounds great. I'm going to use the bathroom real quick."

I turned on the gas and stood in front of the flames, letting the heat soak into my hands. I'd felt perpetually cold since arriving here. The flames entwined in a rhythmic pattern.

"So, I assume this is what the abbey looks like?" Emily asked, breaking my hypnotic stare at the fire.

I spun around. Emily was holding my sketchbook.

"Where did you get that?" I grabbed the pad from her.

"It was on the back seat of the car. I picked it up and carried it in for you. What's with you?"

The pad was open to the last page. I looked at my drawing again. It was the same one of the abandoned building, a stylish sketch that almost looked more like Emily's polished, pre-accident art than my rough drawings.

"Who is that person in the window?" Emily asked.

Person? I scanned the sketch, looking at all the windows until I noticed the round one in the bell tower. The muscles in my neck tensed. A dark figure peeked out from behind the glass.

I stared at the pad. "I didn't draw this, either," I said to myself.

"*Either?* What do you mean?" Emily asked.

I gazed blankly at the drawing, frozen.

"Will, your hands are shaking. What is it?" she asked, her voice rising.

"I don't know. This morning I made some sketches. Originally, I drew a renovated hotel made up to look like the 1890s. I dropped my sketchbook when I saw the girl going into the water and didn't get it back till later. That's when I noticed the drawing had changed."

"Changed like how?"

"The drawing I made isn't here. Just this one of the decrepit abbey. And I did *not* draw a figure standing in the window. That's new even from when I found it. The window was there, but no one in it. At least I didn't see anyone before. And there aren't even windows on that tower. I would've drawn an element as noticeable as that." I grabbed the folder with the photo Lance had given me. It was taken from a different angle, and no windows were visible. I couldn't have gotten the idea from looking at that. I gripped the picture so tightly my fingers started to ache.

Quickly, I scanned my drawing to see if there was anything recognizable in the figure's style of dress. The person was cloaked in shadow, nothing but a pale face and blank eye slits.

Emily wrapped her hand around my arm and pulled me close. "Okay, I think you need to relax and not obsess about blankets and drawings right now."

I closed my eyes, letting her touch sink in. All I saw in my mind's eye was the face of the girl standing on the shore, her glare burning into me, a knife of hatred mixed with sadness.

I leaned away and took a closer look at the drawing. I hadn't lifted a pen to this pad since seeing that woman. Could I have somehow started to draw her in the window and not remembered?

"Look," Emily said, letting me go, "you lost the sketchpad on the beach. Someone found it, maybe drew the sketch, then tossed it back where you found it. It's probably just a—"

"Coincidence?" *Like the blanket?* "This is my pad." I pounded on the sketch paper. "This can't be the work of some random stranger on the beach. That's too convenient."

Wasn't it?

CHAPTER TEN

I must have woken up at least four times that night to check on Emily. I expected a nightmare to drive her out of bed or even back to Seattle. She hadn't said anything after examining the sketch again. In fact, another long, trademark silence between us followed. I wondered how much I'd freaked her out, maybe even made her wary of me.

The day's events kept replaying as I tried to make sense of it all. I was torn between never wanting to see the abbey again and finding out exactly what was going on. Between the drowning and the blanket, Martin's stories, and even Vaughn's complaints about juvenile pranks, Winterbay was cloaked in mystery.

I needed to switch gears. I had a job to do with Ted and James and needed to get them some preliminary sketches. There wasn't much time to impress them.

When I woke up the fourth time, I found Emily still sound asleep. Normally she got up to use the bathroom two or three times. Not tonight.

At least one of us would be rested by tomorrow.

I glanced at the clock, 3:07. I rolled out of bed and stumbled to the desk to work on the drawings and take some Tylenol for my forehead, which was still aching. Using Lance's photo, I re-sketched the abbey as the same 1890s summer wonderland I'd drawn before. Hopefully Ted and James wouldn't think I was some amateurish hack.

"Will?"

I glanced over. Emily was sitting up in bed. "Don't you have a meeting?" she asked groggily. My eyes darted to the alarm clock. It was 6:50. Time had flown.

"Yes, we're supposed to meet around 8:00. Did you sleep well?" I asked.

She stretched. "A little rough, but okay," she said.

"Well, you can have a down day here and just rest and relax," I said.

"I really don't want to be cooped up, and I've been thinking…" she said.

"Oh?" I asked.

"I want to help you," she said.

"Help me with what?"

"That girl," she said. "Finding her. I'd like to help."

An alarm went off in my head. When Emily's friend Ariel was pregnant, she'd wanted to help. After Ariel suffered a miscarriage, Emily beat herself up for not helping enough. She was constantly worried about the baby, money, her hand, many other things, and she always seemed to want to "help" make things better.

It always backfired. It depressed her, frustrated me, and ended in more fighting. I might be intrigued by this nun mystery, even a little scared, but I didn't want Emily obsessed with trying to help find this girl. Besides, what would she do? Go down to the beach and look for a woman washed up along the shore? Or if Vaughn was right, interrogate high school girls?

I wished I hadn't been so rash to bring her here.

"Don't worry about that," I said. "The more I think about it, maybe that cop's idea, that it was a prank, some girl pretending to drown, is right."

"What?" Emily asked. "You never said that last night."

"Well, I didn't want to sound like an idiot, getting fooled."

"Why would someone play a joke like that, faking a drowning?"

I shrugged. "Vaughn says it's a local tradition, on Halloween. Who knows why."

"Yeah, but Halloween is over. Do you really believe the cops?" Emily asked, her eyes narrowed.

"Um, well, I think it's a possibility. They never found a body."

"Will," she said, lowering her voice, "I know you. You aren't buying that."

I shook my head. "Yes, I am. Anyway, let's forget about it. I'll get these drawings to Ted and James and then we can relax, maybe do a little sightseeing. In fact," I continued, "if the meeting goes well, maybe we don't need to stay here at all. We can fly back to Seattle."

"Home? But I just got here," she said. "Besides, can you give them what they want so fast? We really need this project, and I have to tell—"

"No need to worry. These sketches will be great, and I can do the rest from home. It will be fine."

"Fine? Will, the mortgage was late last month. They called before I left to the airport. Why didn't you tell me?"

I guess tearing up the notice hadn't been enough. "Because I'm handling it," I said.

"Mortgage companies don't call when you are 'handling' it."

I ground my teeth. "I think once you start working again, it will all pan out," I said.

"We just talked about me not getting a job right away, remember?"

"I thought you were just thinking about that," I said. "We never really agreed on you not working. Don't you still have an application in with Microsoft?"

Emily shook her head.

"*What*? You pulled the application?" I said, my voice rising.

Emily was silent for a moment. "No, I just haven't heard anything."

Her eyes flicked away. What was she hiding?

"Will, you really shouldn't leave. And don't you think a good word from Ted and James could lead to maybe a raise or a promotion at the firm?"

A job anyway. "I will work it out," I said, crumpling a piece of paper.

"Are you even *listening* to me right now?" Emily asked.

I threw the paper into the wastebasket. "Yes, and I said I'll work it out somehow," I repeated loudly and slowly.

Emily threw her head back. "God, you're not even the same person."

"What is that supposed to mean?" I asked, trying everything within my power not to yell.

A thud hit the window, rattling the panes.

Emily and I looked at each other before we ran to the window.

I drew back the curtains. Close to the top of the pane was a large circular crack, like someone had thrown a rock at the glass.

"Was that a bird?" Emily asked. She peeked outside.

"Must have been," I said. "Unless some kids are playing baseball in the parking lot."

"I hope the bird's not hurt," Emily said.

"I can't see anything. I'm going down there," I said. I didn't particularly want to go outside, but it gave me a good excuse to stop this argument. Putting on my coat, I shut the door and made my way downstairs, walking fast to blow off some steam. I hated fighting.

A dim streetlamp on the side of the hotel lit the parking lot, and it was pointed away from where any bird might have fallen after hitting our window. A light frost iced all the cars. Drawing on what little light I had, I walked up and down the lot a couple of times, half-heartedly looking for our window attacker.

I caught a glimpse of white out of the corner of my eye. Lying half underneath my rental car's front end was a seagull. Its head was twisted at an odd angle with one wing bent completely out of shape. It didn't move as I approached.

The bird's eyes reflected the lamppost light, wide open and staring, lifeless.

I pulled on one of my winter gloves and eyed a dumpster at the far end of the parking lot. I didn't want to drive over this thing. Reluctantly, I reached out. I wasn't the biggest fan of gulls. At the Seattle waterfront, they dive-bombed my French fries.

As soon as I grabbed its wing, my vision went fuzzy. Dark and tunneled, a stark picture of a small wooden motorboat flashed through my mind. It bounced in the mist-covered waves. Overhead, a large flock of seagulls emerged from the fog, swooping perilously close to the boat.

Panicked, I dropped the bird.

As quickly as the pictures had come, they vanished and my vision returned. I stared at the bird.

What the hell was that?

I knew I had flashbacks of the car accident, but no motorcycle was in sight here to trigger me, and these were images I didn't think I'd ever seen before. I tried to remember the entire sea scene. Sometimes doing certain routine actions brought up past events, seemingly unrelated, to mind, but this was more like a seizure. I'd never been lost at sea in a small boat.

Just then the bird's glassy eye locked on me, and a searing pain throbbed in my hand. I jumped back and pulled off my glove. A gash oozed on the back of my hand. Blood ran down my fingers in tiny rivulets of red. I glanced back at the bird. It still lay unmoving on the frosted pavement. Had it just pecked me, through my glove? I'd thought it was dead.

I panted as I backed away. The bird still hadn't moved.

I didn't want to see any more.

I dashed back into the hotel.

"Well?" Emily asked, genuine concern in her voice.

"It was just a bird. A seagull," I said.

Emily's eyes went wide when she spotted my bleeding hand. "Oh my gosh."

She grabbed my arm and led me into the bathroom. Turning on the faucet, she pushed my hand under the water and lathered it with soap. The foaming water mirrored the image of the boat and the sea.

"What happened?"

"Uh," was all I could get out.

"Did the bird do this? I hope this doesn't get infected," Emily said. "Those seagulls are filthy. I hate how close they fly to the crowds down at the waterfront at home."

I grunted again.

"Are you okay? You're acting funny again."

Was I okay?

I shook my head, trying to clear my thoughts.

"Yeah, I'm okay. I think I'm just a little shocked."

Once I was cleaned up, the wound didn't look so bad. Emily had some antibiotic ointment in her purse. Her touch on my hand soothed as she bandaged me. I looked into her eyes.

"Hey, I'm sorry I got angry. This trip has been a lot to handle. I'm staying here, and I promise I'll get the mortgage company straightened out soon, and we'll figure out you not working for a while. Let me make it up to you and take you to breakfast before I have to go."

She hugged me. "Thank you. This means a lot. I'm glad you're going to stay. While you're working, I want to find out what happened to that girl. I doubt it was a prank."

Emily and I grabbed breakfast at a cafe kitty-corner from the Winterbay Public Library. It was a quaint little place with maroon booths mostly filled with what appeared to be regulars—old men sipping coffee and chatting about local news. They gave us unwelcome gazes as we sat at the only open table. I glanced around for Martin, but he wasn't among the early-morning gatherers.

Emily and I took our time eating while I tried not to dwell on the seagull in the parking lot. I didn't have the brainpower to think about its strangeness right now. I kept the conversation as light as possible. My nerves were picking up again, this time because of the sketches. I'd only spent three or so hours on them. They weren't enough to show clients.

"They'll be fine," Emily said, as we walked toward the parking lot. "I saw them, and they really look good. I would tell you if they didn't."

"Thanks, we'll see." I took her hand as we approached the parking lot. "I love you."

"I love you, too," she said, smiling. "I think I'll walk down Main Street for a while and see what there is to see." She glanced at the library. "Maybe I can do some knitting there a little later." She flexed her hand. "Your sweater turned out so well, maybe I'll try another." She smiled and patted her yarn-filled bag, then stopped. "Well, without the heart maybe. That is kind of creepy."

"I'd just as soon forget it," I said.

"Might do some research on the abbey and the drowning too."

"It just happened yesterday," I said. "What could you find online?"

Emily shrugged. "Who knows? Maybe there's a secret cult of drowning nuns they aren't telling us about," she said with a grin.

"Sounds like a plan," I said. I hoped Emily's joking meant she'd spend the day knitting and wouldn't get wrapped up in "helping" solve the mystery of the drowned girl. "I'll pick you up when I'm done, and we'll grab dinner." After giving her a kiss, I set off toward the abbey.

A rush of gravel trucks pulled out of the quarry road and forced me to wait. I was going to sound incredibly lame apologizing for being late in a town where "heavy traffic" was two cars on the road at any given time.

It was nearly 8:30 when I finally pulled up the long narrow driveway, a half-hour late for the meeting. Two cops were getting into their car parked near the stone fountain. One was Officer Vaughn. He walked up to my car. I rolled down the window, eager for any news.

"Just thought I'd tell you that we haven't found anything. No bodies, no reports of missing girls. Nothing."

Why wasn't I surprised?

Vaughn stared at me.

"Um, so what's next?" I asked.

"Well, we'll keep our eyes and ears open," Vaughn said, rubbing his nose and looking off into the distance.

"That's it then?" I asked. "One day and you're finished?"

"Like I said, we'll keep our eyes and ears open. I'll see if anyone at the high school heard about a prank story. Not much else to do."

"Still on the prank thing?" I asked.

"Have to eliminate every possibility," Vaughn said.

"Except the obvious one: that a girl probably died here yesterday."

Vaughn locked his gaze on me. "We haven't found a body, or a single thing that corroborates your story. You know how things are these days. If a girl like you described had gone missing, her picture would be plastered all over the internet by now along with ten thousand whack-job conspiracy theories about how she was taken by submarine aliens or abducted by Mexican drug cartels. None of that has happened. I'd think you'd be glad. After all, isn't it better that no one died?"

He turned and walked back to his car.

I guess we were done.

I glanced around the parking lot. The cop car was the only one in the lot. No sign of anyone else looking for evidence, or even Ted and James' car. Had I missed them? "Hey," I called to Vaughn. "You haven't seen my employers around here, have you?"

"Nope." He jumped into his car and sped off, leaving me alone.

Okay then.

I waited by the car.

Hopefully Ted and James were running late too and hadn't come and gone already.

I crossed my arms, wondering what to make of Vaughn's explanation and what exactly he'd been doing here so early in the morning. It was apparent that the cops weren't going to do anything more, but the vision of that girl's face would haunt me forever.

I looked at my fingers, ticking off one for all the odd things I'd seen. The drowning, the sketches, the girl in the window, the bird.

Was I really hallucinating?

I leaned against the car and held my head. The wind picked up, chilling me along with the fear that something really was wrong with me. I reached into my pocket for my phone.

It was empty. Crap. How could I forget I'd lost it?

I listened to the sounds of the birds tweeting in the forest, and tried to focus on the rugged landscape instead of the paranoid noise in my head. I had a wide panoramic view of the coast. The waves were choppy, and the distant sky the color of gunmetal. So much for a sunny five-day forecast. Martin had been right. A storm was on the way.

A movement down on the beach where the girl had drowned caught my eye. It took all I had to remain calm. I peered closer, willing my pulse to slow. Someone was walking through the tall grass close to where I'd dropped my sketchbook. Vaughn was gone. Was someone else still investigating down there? Maybe it was the girl from yesterday, back to play more games.

I made my way toward the beach. The wind brought a sharper chill, and my breath puffed out white and misty in the air. After stumbling down the ridge at the cliff's edge and making my way over some jagged rocks, I reached the shore and walked toward the figure. "Hello!" I called.

The figure turned around but didn't wave back. As I moved closer, I saw it was an old man scanning the waves and the area around him.

"Excuse me?" I said.

The man shifted toward me. He looked to be in his 70s and had white hair with a yellowish tinge at the ends like he'd smoked most of his life. His face had the tan, weathered quality of leather stretched too tightly. He wore a yellow rain slicker, green wellington boots, glasses, and a blue-and-white striped scarf wrapped around his neck that hung to his knees. A red beret with a pompom on top finished off the eccentric, mismatched look.

"This yours?" he asked in some kind of British accent. He reached into his pocket and took out a phone.

I blinked as he held it out. "Yes! Thank you! I lost it yesterday."

He nodded. "You've missed a few calls."

I checked the missed numbers. Emily, Ted, and a local number I assumed was the police. That was all. I looked up at the tall blades of grass whipping in the wind. I was sure the phone had fallen out of my pocket when I slipped in the water.

"Name's Duncan," he said. His bony hands stayed clasped at his waist.

Duncan? The guy Vaughn and the diver had mentioned yesterday?

"I take care of the lighthouse." He pointed toward the tall spindle with the fading red roof. The spire matched his scarf and cap combination. He shook his head. "Automated. Not much left to do these days except make sure the light don't go out, so I take a lot of walks."

I cleared my throat. "I'm Will Larson. I'm the architect working on the restoration of the abbey. I'm sure you've heard about it."

"Yeah, I heard. Damned fool waste of time." Duncan looked back toward the water. Dark gray clouds, heavy with rain loomed over the bay. "Ain't much of a vacation site," he said with a cough. "Nothing but wind, ice, snow, rain, rocks, and bird droppings. And it ain't safe."

I had to agree with him on that last part. "Did you hear about the drowning yesterday?" I asked.

He continued to stare out over the water. "A storm's coming," he said. "Always a storm this time a year. Not a fit place to be." He tugged on his scarf, tightening it around his neck. The wind picked up and caught the knitted ends, whipping them up into his face.

"Excuse me. I don't mean to be rude, but did you hear of the girl who may have drowned yesterday?" I said, pointing toward the rocks. "I was here when it happened, but I couldn't save her. Did you happen to see anything?"

He shook his head.

"The police," I said, "well, they didn't act too concerned. It seemed so strange. I just wondered if you'd seen or heard something. Maybe she's still alive, and—"

"The cops wouldn't bother now, would they?" Duncan brushed past me and headed up the beach.

I chased after him. "Sorry? Where I come from, the police take drownings seriously."

"You'd better go back to where you came from then," Duncan said. He looked up at the sky. "Don't want to get caught up in the rain. I got a long walk ahead of me."

I stared at him as he quickened his pace, trudging along the pebbled beach. He must have known something about this place. As old as he was, he'd probably been here for ages.

"Wait. The girl," I said. "The one I saw go into the water. It seems like you know this area pretty well. Do you have any idea why a young girl would be out here? The cops think it was a prank. Does that happen often?"

"Prank?" he said with a sneer. "Typical. It's *always* a prank to the cops."

"Then you think I did see a girl drown, a nun?"

At the word "nun" he spun on me. After a moment, he turned away and walked on. I hurried to keep up.

"What?" I asked. "What is it?"

"Nothing."

"But you looked shocked when I said she was a nun. Is that important?"

He hurried, not answering my question.

"Look, I don't even know why I'm saying this to you, but I found my sketchbook…someone drew a picture of this abbey with a figure standing at a window up there," I said, pointing to the bell tower. I think it was the girl I saw drown." I jabbered on, not even making sense to myself.

"Will!" I heard a shout from above.

I looked up. Two men stood on the rocky outcrop waving their hands.

Duncan hurriedly walked north along the shore while the men I assumed to be Ted and James waited.

I watched Duncan march away, wondering what secrets about Winterbay Abbey the old man was keeping.

CHAPTER ELEVEN

I stumbled up to the rocky ridge toward Ted and James.

Hopefully, I could explain what happened yesterday well enough so I wouldn't get fired.

They did not smile at all.

"Sorry we're late. We had to make a stop in town at our office. I'm Ted." The taller and younger of the two men shook my hand. He had a thick mustache and black-rimmed glasses. "And this is my partner, James," he said, handing my palm off.

James was thin, had long downy white-blonde hair. He wore a thick green down-filled coat and tailored jeans rolled at the cuffs. He was maybe ten years older than Ted and looked like he could be a modern-day Elven king. "I have to say that we'd like to know more about what happened here. Having a police presence and a potential scandal on a project we've barely even started is making us question Lance's choice about who he sent to work with us," James said.

If it hadn't been so cold, I probably would have started sweating.

James looked at my forehead.

"Uh, I assure you I had nothing to do with what happened," I said. "I just happened to be here." I recounted everything, filling them in on the local pranks as well.

As I reached the end of my story, their expressions softened a little.

"Well, that's not good to hear," James said, crossing his arms.

I still hadn't convinced him. "I apologize for the door being left wide open. Honestly, I was so scared, I just jumped in the car to go find help," I said.

"That's completely understandable," Ted said. He nudged James. "I do have to say the whole thing is bizarre. It seems a little too soon for the police to have given up the search and assumed no one has died."

"That's exactly what I thought," I said, nodding.

"Well, let's hope that the police get this figured out soon," James said. "Problems with the cops can cost a lot of money."

Ted snorted. "Stop worrying. Maybe we can profit from the local legends."

I was grateful when he smiled, but felt they were still uncertain about me.

James rolled his eyes at Ted. "Yeah, maybe. Let's focus on what we know has the potential of actually bringing in money." He gestured toward the abbey.

A cold wind whipped around us. James shivered. "Come on. Those of us with low thyroid function don't have the body heat to brave the elements," he said.

We made our way toward the building and went inside. "Quite a place, isn't it?" Ted asked as he gazed around the large windowed room I'd imagined as the restaurant and lounge. "You can see from just a quick look why we loved this place. The sea is so mighty and unrestrained here."

James cleared his throat. "We are in the wild here, and with a hotel it will be a safe haven in the wilderness. And a profitable one," he added, wiggling his eyebrows. "That lighthouse is a million-dollar bonus, and for free. Everyone loves to look at lighthouses. Maybe we could even have boat tours."

"I agree," I told them. "The building needs some work…well, a lot of work. You'll want a new, efficient HVAC system, and I'm sure the wiring and plumbing are out of code and damned near useless. I haven't had time to check for infestations or mold or—"

Ted shook his head. "Yes, yes, we know all that. That's not why we brought you here. We're bringing in a mechanical engineer in a bit."

"I like to make certain my plans will work before I let a mechanical engineer tell me I have to tear down walls to make their pet HVAC system fit."

"Well, that's something I can appreciate," James said. "Efficiency and going the extra mile."

My neck muscles relaxed a bit.

"What we truly want from you, though," Ted looked back at me, "is the dream. We want to see what *you* see in this place, and we want *our* dreams put into drawings that money can turn into reality."

In the distance, an explosion crackled through the trees. Both Ted and James winced.

"We've been assured the quarry is nearing its end," Ted said. "It will only be running long enough to supply the needs for our project, road gravel mostly. Hopefully, that's true and not another thing to add to our list of worries."

James nodded, but a frown remained on his face when he looked at me.

I cleared my throat and pulled out my drawings. They were far from detailed, but at least I'd been able to do both interiors and exteriors. Hopefully they'd be enough to get my ideas about the project through to them.

A lot of people at my firm just opened up a laptop and went through 3D renderings during client meetings. Of course I would put some of those together as well. Call me old-fashioned, but I liked pen drawings to be the first view. That was one of the things Lance liked about my style when he hired me.

Ted and James sat at an old leaning table with a cracked top. They studied the drawings, muttering and whispering to each other in tones so hushed I couldn't make out a word.

"Give us a moment," James said.

I tried to keep my nerves at bay. While I waited, I wandered back outside into the cold. I didn't care if it was freezing.

I started pacing, trying to distract myself.

I thought back to the original sketch that morphed into the creepy present-day abbey. It still didn't make sense. Maybe Emily was right about someone picking up my lost notebook and doing their own sketch. It seemed unlikely, but I thought of Duncan. Could he have a skill with illustration and just couldn't pass up the opportunity? Although he had found my phone and was certainly a strange guy, the chances were slim.

I banished thoughts of Duncan as I glanced up at the bell tower. It was still very early in the pre-design phase, but I'd already imagined an observation room there, maybe with a telescope for couples enjoying a drink while looking at the sea or the stars. The oculus window from the mystery drawing was a good idea. I might work it in somehow. Emily would like that.

A stinging northeast wind picked up. I shivered and then completely froze when I looked at the tower again. A fleeting reflection glared off a windowpane. I blinked again to make certain I wasn't imagining things. There was no question—the same window from the drawings was there. And…

My entire body went numb.

The pale face of a woman looked out through the glass.

I closed my eyes. My hands grew clammy as I clenched my fists and breathed deeply. *No, this is impossible.* "She is not there," I said. "No one is there."

"Who's not there?"

I opened my eyes. Ted and James stood under the archway looking at me.

I took a quick glance at the tower. Only worn brick. No window. No face. "Uh, nothing," I said rather shakily and embarrassed.

Ted nodded, and I followed them back inside, trying to calm my raging fears.

"Well, I have to say a 19th century European hotel isn't what I'd imagined. I was thinking more of some lobster palace monstrosity. You've really set me straight," Ted said.

I looked at James to see if he agreed.

"Absolutely," he said. "Wonderful concepts. Large enough to pay for the expense of setting up here but small enough to still be intimate. In fact, we were wondering…" he turned to Ted.

"We were wondering," Ted continued with casual ease, "given your taste for this particular style, if you'd consider working on several more projects we're eyeing. We can't go into too many details, but we've been in contact with a major hotel chain. They have some big plans to branch out and start a line of independent resorts with an Old-World kind of charm. We have been searching high and low for someone who can design that style, to no avail. It's been over a year-long quest to find an architect with the right vision. I can't tell you how lucky we feel you've been dropped in our lap like this. We'd like to call your firm and have them put you on the assignment. These drawings," Ted said, holding up my sheets, "are perfect for what the chain is imagining."

I stopped, glancing back and forth between the both of them. Two minutes ago, I thought I was on the verge of being fired.

"The chain is quite clear that they are committed to buying old properties in downtowns, revival areas, and renovating them," James said. "It would be all renovation work, which seems to be up your alley."

"And each one unique," Ted concluded. "A dozen hotels all over the country, and no two alike." He waved his arms up and down. "Each would be a special project all its own, with different challenges and possibilities. You'd have multiple opportunities to come up with the visions like what you've done here."

I wasn't sure what to say. Hopefully, I wasn't hallucinating. They'd just described my dream job. I'd never done anything on that scale before. "What chain are we talking about?"

"Well," Ted said, a sneaking look in his eyes, "we can't say at this point. Their name may start with a giant 'W' though."

I could think of several "Ws" out there, each richer than the one before. This was too good to be true.

"We can talk more about those projects later. Of course for now, we'll want more detailed renderings, and we've got our own thoughts on the renovation here," James said. He looked at Ted.

"But those are details you can work on for the next month while you're here," Ted said.

My stomach dropped.

"Month?" I asked. "I thought we were only going to be here for a week, and then I'd finish the project in Seattle."

"Well," James said, "we're going to be here a while longer, and we prefer to work closely with the architect. Call me old-fashioned, but I hate this distance online thing. Don't worry about expenses. We'll pay for everything, including your wife if she wants to come out."

"She's actually here now. She decided to join me for the week, but I'm not sure if you know she's pregnant. She needs her own doctor." And maybe I did too.

Ted scratched his chin. "Hmm, you'll need a better place to stay than a hotel. And of course we'll make sure to have the best doctor here take care of her. We will also make sure both of you get back home when she needs to. She's not due immediately, is she?"

I shook my head. "She's four and a half months along."

"Wonderful," Ted said. "Then it's agreed."

I nodded and rubbed the back of my neck. Things were moving so fast.

"Uh. Of course," I said, trying to sound as enthusiastic as possible.

"Great," Ted and James said at the same time.

I forced a smile.

CHAPTER TWELVE

Ted and James headed back to town, leaving me with promises of getting Emily and me a rental house and an appointment with Winterbay's top obstetrician, if there even was such a person in a town this size. I wasn't sure Emily would be up for staying so long, but she'd be beyond thrilled with the news.

Ted and James wanted to meet tomorrow over dinner and talk more in-depth about the plans. Given that time frame, I had to scope around the abbey to get the interior details as well as the mechanical systems. I would do my job quickly, leave fast, and spend a nice, quiet evening with Emily. Maybe I could find the nicest restaurant in Winterbay. There was considerable cause for celebration.

I headed back to the courtyard. The bell tower poked its head through a small patch of fog.

No sign of any pale-faced woman.

I'd imagined the whole thing.

The outside wall of the tower stood blank. No window, barely even room to fit one.

I must have been getting my ideas for the renovation confused with what I was actually seeing. That window was my idea, it had to be. I must have made those sketches, but forgotten about them while worrying over the girl and everything else.

Okay, enough.

I'd just been handed the biggest opportunity of my career. If it worked out, I wouldn't have to worry about money. *Put the mysteries aside, and get to work on some new drawings, Larson.*

I went back inside and up the stairs to the top floor toward the bell tower. I needed to check out the possibility of adding a window and using the tower space for an observation room, and maybe prove to myself that I wasn't crazy.

The hall was dark, unlit, empty.

I walked to the end, the sound of my footsteps echoing against the cold, peeling walls. I reached the door to the large room where I'd found the baby blanket. As I put my hand on the knob, I paused, waiting.

Something didn't feel right.

I took my palm off the handle. Then back on. *It's just an entrance to a room. Get a grip.*

I opened the door quickly.

A flash of white caught my eye a split second before a loud fluttering shook the air like a windstorm. I cried out, throwing my arm over my face as the roar of flapping wings passed over me. Birds flew in a frenzy down the hall, swirling about in a mad, panicked escape.

I lay flat on the floor, my breathing and pulse racing. The birds continued to beat their wings in a flurry, bouncing off the walls and battering the door frame. The sound was deafening. They returned, swooping over me, squawking. Their wings smacked my head as they passed.

Then they were gone. The flapping of wings was replaced by the gentle sound of a breeze flowing in through the broken window on the far side of the room. All that remained was a scattering of feathers on my jacket.

Where had they gone? The window had been broken since my last visit, but the fist-sized opening was hardly large enough to allow so many birds to exit in such a short time. In fact it didn't look large enough to have let them in. Perhaps they had flown down the stairs and were now creating havoc throughout the rest of the building.

Great.

But how had they gotten inside?

I listened. If they were still in the building, they made no sound.

I caught my breath and sat up, leaning against the doorway, straining to hear.

Silence.

And I had worried about rats.

I took a deep breath and stood back up.

The floor was covered with a thick layer of dust, the residue of years of abandonment.

Apart from my footprints from the day before, the dust was undisturbed, and there were no droppings. Even if the birds had just been passing through, they'd have left far more nasty evidence of their presence.

I put my hand on my forehead as a sharp spike of pain settled in my temples. I popped two Tylenol from my pocket.

Okay, let it go. They were just birds, probably escaping the cold.

I took a deep breath and walked to the window. I'd seen this one from outside, but it was at a lower level than the tower. I pulled on the rusted metal latch. Red dust fell onto my hand as I forced the window open. It creaked as I pushed it out into the now dense and dripping fog. I leaned out. The fog shrouded the entire coast, like the inside of a cloud. I could hardly see the rocky beach below.

I craned my neck. The tower's brick walls were rough and losing their mortar, but uninterrupted by any windows above me.

As I pulled my head back inside, the bell in the tower suddenly clanged. Once, twice, three times. My stomach knotted. There was no one there to ring it.

Or was there?

A deep cold settled into my chest.

I thought of those kids and their pranks. Could they be up to this after having pulled off a fake drowning? If that was true, they certainly went to great lengths for a joke. And what about Duncan? He was familiar with the nunnery and probably walked the grounds often. He didn't like the idea of a hotel, and living here for so long, he would know all the stories, the ones the kids told. Maybe he was trying to scare me away and prevent the hotel from being built.

That or the abbey had its own hunchback manning the tower.

The idea of being run off by Duncan gave me a new sense of urgency. I wasn't going to let some fossilized lighthouse keeper stop me from my project.

Turning on my flashlight, I walked back into the hall and looked for the doorway leading to the tower. I counted the doors: eight. All bedrooms with decrepit beds and chairs. I shook my head. There had to be a way up there. How else could you get to the bell?

I didn't remember seeing a door inside the room I'd just left, but the tower was just above. A door should be there along with a staircase. I walked back inside. The temperature had dropped quickly from the open window, and my breath formed a fog nearly as thick as the mist outside.

The beam from my light flicked across the room. I scanned the walls looking for a door and checked the ceiling in case there was a trapdoor. Nothing. The walls, covered with cracked yellow wallpaper, showed no evidence of another entrance.

The bell rang again. Three peals. I could feel the reverberations coming through the ceiling and vibrating the floor beneath my feet. A small chip of paint fell from the ceiling, landing on my head. I shined the light up and for the first time noticed a crack in the plaster. Not the jagged break of an old stressed ceiling, but straight, like it had been drawn with an edge. Grabbing a chair, I climbed up and shone my light along the break. More plaster broke and fluttered down to the floor. Reaching up, I snagged the remainder and pulled it loose. I spotted the loop of a handle.

I grabbed the handle and pulled down. A trapdoor opened with a *crack* and spray of plaster dust. A ladder attached to the trapdoor slid to the floor. The sound of my pulse in my ears was deafening.

"Duncan!" I shouted.

He had to be in the tower, and there had to be another way up. This ladder hadn't been lowered since it had been plastered over, decades ago.

After a moment's hesitation, I stepped onto the ladder and climbed up onto a solid wooden floor, in better condition than the one below. The space was just large enough for the base of a set of wrought-iron winding stairs that ascended to another floor. These were covered with dust even thicker than in the bedrooms. Cobwebs hung dense from the walls and ceiling.

Where was the other entrance?

The bell rang again. One, two, three. Much louder here. The ringing sent shock waves undulating through the abandoned spider webs like strings of a harp.

Brushing them out of my way, I climbed the steps and pushed open another trapdoor. It banged onto the floor above with a crash, sending a torrent of dust swirling into the air, caught in my light like stars. I coughed and sputtered as the residue of decades of neglect tickled my lungs.

The heavy sense that someone, or something, waited for me sent chills through my whole body.

"Duncan?" I called. "Are you up here?"

There was no answer. I shined the beam upwards and spotted the bell rope hanging limp and unmoving. I followed the line of the rope until the light caught the dull surface of the cracked bell above.

Who had rung it?

To my right, a slight creak broke the silence. I spun and pointed the flashlight. There was another door a few feet away. It looked like the entrance to a broom closet, but had an old rusted padlock hanging from a latch. The door was ajar, the bottom tracing an arc through the dust.

"Duncan!" I shouted. "Damn you! Stop playing games and come out."

Still no answer.

No light came from behind the door. If Duncan was there, he was hiding alone in the dark, waiting.

My pulse quickened again as I began to wonder if Duncan wasn't just a prankster, but a dangerous nutjob. How far would he go to scare me away?

I should have left then, come back with the police, or at least Ted and James, but a curiosity I wished I'd left in childhood pushed me on. I walked up the final two steps and over to the door.

I pointed the light inside. The room was a rectangle about six feet by ten, tiny, hardly more than a closet. No one was there. On the far wall, my light caught the pane of a circular window, the glass dusty and dark.

So there had been a window here.

Through the dirt, I made out brickwork. I walked over, and pulling open the frame, gave the bricks a hard rap with the butt of my flashlight. The mortar disintegrated, and one of the bricks inched out from the wall. I scratched out the remaining mortar, nothing but dust now, and leaned in. Two bricks fell away and clattered onto the ground below.

Fog now filled the view. I could just make out the beach and sea beyond through the hole.

I took a deep breath. Perhaps I'd subconsciously noticed a mismatch in the brickwork outside after all, and it made me think of covered windows. That had to be it. My trained mind must have noticed the faint outline of a lintel, and I filled in the blanks without thinking about it. That and my "design mode" must have had me imagining future guests in this window. It was the only explanation.

I pulled the window closed and sighed.

As I stepped back, I noticed a small handprint on the glass, embedded in the dust. It looked as though someone had leaned against the pane many years ago to look out.

I swallowed. The crude imprint had a soft, delicate aspect that made me think of Emily, of how her hand had been so soft, so skilled, so fine. Until that night.

I turned away and studied the rest of the space. Sitting at the back was a rocking chair. A floorboard had been ripped up under the chair. I shined my flashlight into the hole. It was empty. Next to where the floorboard was, an iron bed, like those in the rooms below, stood near a tiny cradle. I inspected it more closely. The cradle had a thin dusty mattress, stained and threadbare. Above it hung a handmade paper mobile of tiny birds. The folded paper had been colored green and yellow, now dim with age, and each bird had an eye that seemed to stare directly at me as the mobile swung gently from the breeze caused by my movement. I could almost feel the beat of their wings and hear their squawks as the birds circled above the tiny bed.

What in the world was a cradle doing here?

I thought of the hand that had left that impression on the window, lovingly crafting these birds for the occupant of the cradle. An overwhelming sadness and sense of loss overcame me as I watched the birds. *Had a child really been living in this hidden room*? Was the handprint the mother's? All behind a padlocked door of a room the size of a cell?

My mind raced to my unborn child. A wave of loneliness washed over me, a pain so extreme I was crushed by isolation. I gasped, my breathing shallow and halting. I leaned over to try to stop the swirling in my head.

After a moment of forced, deep breaths, I calmed myself enough to stand upright. The intense aloneness refused to leave. It was not a fear of dying, but of never being loved again, living a life without a single human contact. I floated in a sea of desolation and abandonment.

Please, Emily, forgive me.

Where was this coming from?

As I stood up, the beam of my flashlight passed over the rocking chair and the pathetic mobile. I hadn't noticed it before, but lying on the seat was a small, round ball that topped a short blue-striped wooden handle. I gently picked it up. Tiny beads inside the ball rattled softly as my hands trembled. Starting at the top of the rattle, tiny teeth marks imprinted every inch of the soft wood. The indentations formed an odd pattern of wavy bites, resembling a puppy's chew toy.

My hand squeezed on its own, locking in a tight grip. I had to force my fingers open. I threw what could only be my childhood rattle to the far side of the room. I nearly fell trying to get to the stairs.

Then I heard it.

I couldn't stop myself from turning around. In the beam of my light, the tiny cradle rocked gently.

My body stood limp from terror. Then a strange noise filled the air. Almost like the sound of a tuning fork. On the other side of the room, I caught the outline of a dark figure standing near the wall. It moved, and I thought my heart would stop. "Who is that?!" I called out. The shadow stopped. I blinked, and pointed my flashlight at it.

There was nothing there. Only empty space. Whatever it was had gone, and the cradle had stopped rocking.

CHAPTER THIRTEEN

Adrenaline raced through me, providing an almost inhuman speed to flee the building. I scrambled down the bell tower's stairs and raced out of the abbey. I floored the rental car, sending up a spray of mud and gravel as I shot toward town.

My clothes, now damp with sweat, clung. Shivering, I blasted the heater as beads continued to dew on my forehead. Flash images of the cradle, the dark figure, and my rattle reeled through my mind while the toll of the abbey's bell continued to ring in my head. *It's okay. Everything's okay. You're fine. It's all okay. There's an explanation. There has to be.*

But what explanation could there be? First, how on Earth had my rattle gotten into that room? I had thrown it away on the other side of the country. Hadn't I? I thought back to the night I came home and found my mother's keepsakes on the couch. I'd taken my rattle out of the trash and handed it to Emily. What had she done with it?

It seemed impossible, but had I somehow brought the rattle I'd found to the abbey? No. That was absolute craziness. What was I even saying?

In almost no time, I reached the library's tiny parking lot. I hurried up the steps flanked by two stone lions and barreled through the door.

I frantically scanned the room. A man sat behind a desk sorting books. He glanced up from his computer monitor. His frown made me wonder what I looked like.

"Will?" I spotted Emily sitting in an overstuffed chair, holding her knitting. She waved, and the librarian gave her a "Be quiet!" look with his index finger on his lips.

I ran to her. Just seeing her alive and well relieved some of my frenzied state.

She looked closer at my face and stood up. "Will? My god, what's wrong *now*?"

I hugged her.

She squeezed me back. "Will?"

After holding her for what seemed like hours, I finally sputtered, "I don't know what's happening."

A woman sitting behind the information desk threw us an irritated look.

"Come on," I said, taking Emily's hand. I led her to the car. As soon as we were inside, I cranked the heater.

I glanced at her belly, wondering what I should even tell her. Who knew the emotional toll this was taking on her, and in turn, our child. I looked up. Her face was covered in shadow, and she was leaning against the door, almost like she was readying herself to jump out of the car if she needed to. I put my head in my hands. "Do you think I'm crazy? Or sick?"

"Why don't you tell me what happened first," she said.

As calmly as I could, I started from the beginning, including the part about my new job offer.

Emily beamed until I got to the part about my trip to the bell tower, the ringing bells, the cradle, the rattle, and the shadow in the corner.

"Are you sure you aren't letting your imagination get the best of you?" she asked, her eyes narrowed in concern. "The abbey is a big, dark place." She reached into her yarn bag and rubbed something between her fingers, as though warming her hands. "You know old buildings as well as anyone. They creak, and things move as they settle. Maybe the bell was stuck and just happened to work itself loose, or maybe those birds disturbed it, or you pulled on the rope by mistake. If the floor sagged a tiny bit when you walked on it, that could rock the cradle. Plus, weird shadows show up all the time. It's not that mysterious. There has to be a logical explanation."

"But that rattle," I said. "How did it get there?"

She shook her head. "That's the least mysterious. Those things go with cradles." She smiled and patted my hand like I was a frightened child.

"It was identical. I know it was. Especially the teeth marks."

She sniffed. "Will, all babies chew. You can't tell one from another. And we did throw it away. Remember?"

An image sprang up of Emily telling me that we didn't need the rattle. She *had* dumped it back in the trash.

I sat back, rubbing my face. "How could it be *here* then?" I asked.

"Because it's not the same one. It just *looks* the same," she said, shaking her head again. "You really are sleep deprived."

"The birds," I said. "The sketch. Where is all of this coming from? I didn't make them up. You saw the drawing, the figure in the window."

Emily shrugged. "We talked about that. Someone else drew it. What I really want to know is why babies would be living at an abbey in the first place. Do you think the baby who lived in that tower was okay? Who was the mother?"

The whirring in my mind paused, struck by her question. Magically transported toys, bells ringing on their own, a drowning girl who didn't exist, and my own possible madness seemed of greater significance to me than whose baby lived at the abbey. "Emily, I don't know and I don't care. That was a long time ago. Worrying about it now is pointless. Forget it. We're going back to the hotel room, and I'm booking our flights home."

"No!" Her voice was sharp, cutting. "You can't run away like that and just let this opportunity with Ted and James go. It's too huge. We have too much to lose."

"I do *not* care!" I put my hands on the steering wheel.

Emily put her hand over mine. Her face strained as she squeezed my fist with her weakened fingers.

"You're really more worried about money than my sanity?!"

"Will, I'd wanted to tell you this earlier...in a happier context...over a romantic dinner, during a sunset or something, but this trip has been nothing but bizarre."

I looked over at her, trying to gauge what she was about to say.

"The day before you left, I had an appointment with Dr. Ellis. She saw something on the ultrasound.... Something she missed before."

"What? You look pretty pregnant to me," I said.

"It's twins," she said.

My hands went cold, and a lump grew in my throat. I put my head on the steering wheel as the world spun around me. "What?" I said, more to myself than to her. "How the hell did she miss that?! That's like Columbus missing the New World."

"This is why I didn't really want to go back to work now. I don't know if I could manage twins and a job right this moment. I…. My mom said she's going to help us in any way she can. Please try not to worry," she said.

"How is she going to help us, Emily? She isn't a millionaire. We are about to lose our damn house!" I yelled.

Emily leaned back, her expression downcast. She pulled her hand away and slid it back inside her knitting bag.

I put my hand on my forehead and sighed. It wasn't like me to yell. "God, I'm sorry. I just…I mean, how are we going to put two kids through college? We're still trying to climb out of our own student loan debts," I said, knowing how lame I sounded.

"Could you be any *more* insensitive right now?! It's not like I can control this! I didn't tell you that night when you came home because I wanted this to be happy news, unlike the first time around. You'd just lost your account, and I didn't want to upset you. I even tried to call you at work right after the appointment, but your phone went straight to voicemail. All I wanted was one small piece of joy in all this," she said.

My chest burned with guilt. I took her hand.

She pulled it away again and turned toward her window. "I'm not ready for this," she said in a low tone. "You have no idea how terrified I was when the pregnancy test came up positive. I'm scared to be a mother. I don't know what I'm doing, and I'm terrified that I'm going to screw this up. What happens if I drop them both because of this hand?" She held it in front of her face, trying to force her fingers to close. After a moment, she hid it again in her knitting.

"Emily, please don't say that."

"All I want is my life back! My life before the accident. I can't do the things I used to do. The things I love. I'm so depressed, Will. The sadness is crushing me more every day. You're not the same either. You have become more and more indifferent. Our relationship is probably never going to be the same again. I feel like you've quit on us, just like you want to quit everything else. Maybe we need to think about…" she said, her voice trailing off.

My chest caved, pulling almost all the breath out of me, as I realized my nightmare of our marriage crumbling was a reality.

"Stop right there," I said. "Don't even think it. I'm not quitting on you, on us. In fact, I'm doing all of this for us. This place, that abbey. I'm doing everything in my power to make a good life for us. I just don't want you here is all. That's why I want to go home."

"So you say."

I gestured toward her. "So, what? You really think I'm making this stuff up? Everything I've seen in the abbey is just an excuse to get out of here?" I sputtered.

"No," she said, hollow and unconvincing. "But…"

"But what?"

She shook her head and looked away.

The coolness in the air brought a clarity to my thoughts. My next words had to be as good as any I had ever chosen. "Look, I realize I may have been acting odd lately, but only because this entire trip has really shaken me up. I think the stress of everything has made me snappy and irritable. I'm trying to do everything I can to support you. And I promise you I'm going to keep doing that and whatever else it takes to make this work. My commitment to you is stronger than the day I married you. I also haven't wanted to say this, but I'm just as scared as you, about the baby, babies. The future."

"That's been more than obvious," she said coolly.

"Just…please, Emily. I love you, and that's why I want to leave. To get you, and me, and *our* babies, away from this situation."

"Just stop making excuses! I need you to get a grip!" Emily yelled.

I sat back and swallowed.

She was right.

I had to get through this project. In fact, I had no choice. I was about to lose everything and trying to get back to Seattle right this minute was probably not the answer.

I took her hand.

She continued to stare out the window.

I hung my head.

She looked over at me. "I need you, Will. More than ever. Please."

I rubbed my watery eyes. "Yes, I'm so sorry. I promise."

Her bad hand twitched in mine.

She looked into my eyes, and then she hugged me.

We held each other as we listened to the traffic go by.

My head pounded as I put the car in reverse. Emily's words cut deep, and all I wanted to do was crawl into bed with her, hold her, and not wake up for a year. I didn't know how much more I could take.

"Hold on," Emily said. "I just thought of something. I didn't do any research like I planned. How about we do some investigating? We can look through newspaper archives on the history of the abbey and get more information. Maybe there are some answers for us here. They might help you in some way."

"How?"

"Maybe there's a history to all this strangeness, a reason the cops don't care about drowned girls at the abbey."

I glanced at the library sign. I felt like I'd just been through a war. If I was tired before, I was on the verge of exhaustion now. The last thing I wanted was more work. Though if I was going to stay and go through with the project, I needed as much information as I could about what I was dealing with.

I'd much rather do research in the hotel. However, Emily was probably on to something. Many newspapers didn't supply their entire history of articles online, and the Wi-Fi in the hotel left much to be desired. It made sense to do the searching here.

In five minutes, Emily and I were standing in front of the male librarian I'd first seen when I came in. He handed me a slip of paper. "This is the password to access our catalog of newspaper articles. What are you looking for exactly?"

"Anything on Winterbay Abbey," I said.

He stopped for a moment, squinting his eyes, then with a sigh said, "You're not ghost hunters, are you?"

"What?" I asked.

He shook his head. "The kids in this town are obsessed with the legends out there. It's a big Halloween tradition. Lots of terribly written research papers."

"So we've heard," Emily said. She glanced sideways at me, a glint in her eye. "What kind of legends?"

"Stories of hauntings out there are as old as the first settlers, even older. The Native Americans have their own tales," he said.

I nodded. "I heard some of that. Shipwrecks, ghost sailors, and such."

"Exactly. And the abbey of course. For some reason, nuns are the perfect subject for ghost stories. They're kind of mysterious.

Must be the way they dress." He chuckled. "Nonsense, of course. But no one listens to me."

I cracked a weak smile. "Well, I'm working on a restoration project, and I just thought I'd see what I could find about the building, old photos, things like that."

"I heard about that project," the librarian said. "Sounds like a great addition to the town. I hope it goes well."

"Me too," I told him, giving Emily a look. At least *someone* here wanted the abbey restored.

I gave Emily the piece of paper. "How far back do the articles go?" I asked.

"Early 1900s. Most of the articles are from the *Winterbay Gazette*. That paper started around 1830. It's only been digitized for the past century though," he said. "The rest is on microfilm."

"Thanks," I said. "This should do the job."

Emily and I made our way toward the desktop computer the man had pointed to.

"Well, I guess someone had to finally say it," Emily said under her breath.

"Say what?"

"Ghosts."

I looked at her. "Don't bring those shows you watch into this. Like you said in the car, there's a logical explanation."

"I may have been playing a little bit of devil's advocate. Besides, just a minute ago you were freaking out about how dangerous it was out at the abbey, and how you couldn't understand what was happening. Ghosts really *are* the most logical explanation."

Logical explanation? Emily had always been drawn to the supernatural, especially angels, although I'd always thought it was mostly fun, watching pseudoscientists hunting spooks or talking about her dad looking over her from above. She'd seemed even more interested lately. Maybe because Ariel had lost her baby?

"I'm still not sure it isn't pranks," I said. "And there's that Duncan guy. He might be behind this. He didn't seem to want a hotel at the abbey. He could be trying to scare me off."

"You never said that before," Emily said. "Why are you backpedaling?"

"I…" I wrung my hands. "Back at the abbey, I was convinced Duncan was behind it, until the rocking cradle and that rattle. And your explanation of the building settling makes sense. That makes Duncan the most likely explanation for the rest."

Emily pursed her lips. "Uh huh, well…Duncan must be a powerful wizard if he can do everything you described."

"That's still more likely than a ghost."

Emily crossed her arms. "We'll see."

Great. Something else to argue about.

A dialogue box prompted us for the password. As soon as I typed it in, a search box popped up.

Emily typed in "Winterbay Abbey." Tons of hits appeared, the latest a small note about Ted and James buying the property.

"Let's see about these Halloween pranks," I said.

Emily nodded and narrowed the search. Thirty or so articles appeared. The kids really had been busy.

"This is all harmless stuff," I said after scrolling through the headlines and reading a handful of reports. "Looks like they were having fun, actually. See, these girls just dressed up like nuns and held a séance twenty years ago."

I skimmed through more stories. The pranks officer Vaughn had complained about were small mentions of kids caught in the woods nearby the abbey, lighting bonfires, drinking beer, and darkly—or comically—summoning spirits of the long-dead. Odd that it was usually girls conducting the strange chanting rituals. Boys seemed simply to have brought the beer. There was nothing rising to the level of pretend drownings or attempts to scare away developers with self-ringing bells and creepy scenes in tower rooms. I wanted more details. It would have been good to know what those kids were interested in up there.

"Wait," Emily said as she spotted another article. "Says here that a girl died ten years ago on Halloween. Killed in a car crash coming from the abbey at night. Her car slid off the road on her way back to town and ended up in the water. Ugh. Sank with her inside. How awful."

I shivered, remembering how cold the water was, and the bleak images of our own car accident. What must that have been like, slowly sinking into the ice-cold bay, frantically trying to get out of a car in blackness as the air slowly seeped away?

Emily scanned down further. There was another death notice. "Look, this girl, back in 1992, after a Halloween bonfire, lost her way and tripped in the dark. She fell off the cliff onto the rocks at high tide right by the abbey. They found her floating in the surf." She glanced at me. "Maybe those pranks aren't as harmless as we've been told."

I nodded, still unsure. "Car crash, falling off a cliff. That's tragic, but hardly evidence of a ghost. Kids get hurt all the time screwing around on Halloween, or anytime for that matter."

Emily scowled. "I don't think that's the cause of what you've been seeing, but maybe those girls saw the same thing as you."

I sighed. "Maybe, but these traditions are a great cover for someone like Duncan to do some dirty work. Hide your malicious intents behind harmless fun and the occasional accident. See if there's anything on Duncan."

A search for his first name, as we didn't know his last, turned up nothing. The lighthouse was mentioned on occasion, but mostly as a backdrop to unrelated issues, or questions of its ongoing usefulness.

"Well," I said. "This isn't helping much. Let's look more into the abbey itself."

"Yeah, good call," Emily said.

An arm's-length list of stories appeared. "Let's start from the beginning," I said. Emily paged forward until we'd reached the very first article about the building's dedication in 1915.

After that, the abbey wasn't too newsworthy. New Mother Superiors were noted. They all pretty much died on their feet, fulfilling their vows. Nothing of interest. The most recent was dated 1962. The headline read, "Winterbay Abbey Prepares for Unexpected Funeral." It was about an abbess who'd had a bad fall and died.

"Crap, I don't see anything," I said. "None of this helps. I can't believe kids are trying to raise nuns from the dead."

"Why don't you type in 'nun' and 'drowning,'" Emily said.

"At least that would tell us if they covered my report," I said. "Although I never saw a reporter or talked to one."

I typed in "nun, Winterbay Abbey, drowning."

"Look," Emily said, pointing at the screen.

The second result read, "Young Nun Succumbs to Drowning Accident." I clicked the link and scanned the article:

> *A young nun, identified as Novitiate Pamela Mayo, drowned during a storm early Thursday night. The woman was a resident of Winterbay Abbey. Police detective Richard Grant stated that Mayo had been out for a walk on the beach and somehow was swept into the sea. Her body was recovered by a boat from the*

Winterbay lighthouse. Funeral arrangements have not been made public.

"Hey, it mentions the lighthouse," I said. "That's a possible connection to Duncan." I checked the date next to the article: February 1, 1961.

Emily enlarged a black-and-white photo at the top of the page. A cold sweat broke out over my entire body. A young girl wearing a nun's habit stared out, serious and unsmiling. The quality of the photograph was faded and poor. Her look of vicious malevolence was absent, but I'd recognize the face anywhere.

Pamela Mayo was the nun I'd seen on the beach.

CHAPTER FOURTEEN

I stared unblinking at the screen, my hands shaking. "I saw her on the beach," I said. "That's her. That's the girl."

"The one you saw drown?" Emily leaned in for a closer look.

"This is crazy," I said.

We sat in silence.

A million thoughts whirled through my mind.

"Well, I guess that explains why they didn't find a body," Emily said. She took my hand. "You're cold as ice."

I took the mouse and clicked "print," then scrolled through the rest of the search results, frantically scanning each headline. There had to be something here to tell me the woman I had seen drown really wasn't a ghost.

Most of what I found were follow-up articles about Pamela Mayo's drowning. I clicked to the next page. At the top, was an article headed, "Winterbay Abbey Met with Second Drowning: Closure Inevitable?" The date read March 10, 1964. Emily and I leaned in closer.

> *Winterbay Abbey was struck this weekend with its second drowning victim in just three years. Seventeen-*

year-old Helen Kelly's remains were found washed ashore after she went missing on March 9th. The previous drowning at the nunnery of nun Pamela Mayo in 1961 had shaken the small community. Both deaths are blamed on high tides and poor weather conditions.

Local officials are now speculating whether this tragedy, combined with financial difficulties, will lead to a closure of the historic building. The Sisters of Immaculate Conception, headquartered in Boston, who run the abbey, have so far made no comment on the matter, but there is conjecture that the abbey's mission has become outdated, and these tragedies only add to the desire to close the site.

Official funeral arrangements for Kelly have not been announced.

An additional black-and-white photo accompanied this article. The picture showed another smiling woman wearing a nun's habit. Her expression was soft, approachable—the exact opposite of Pamela's.

"Wow, she's very pretty," Emily said. "How sad."

"Outdated mission? I wonder what that means," I said.

Emily shrugged. "You don't see nuns around like you used to. I think they're kind of passé now."

I nodded and flicked the mouse to check the results further down the page. Seemed that Winterbay Abbey had its fair share of fatalities. Three nuns had all fallen to their deaths, two down a flight of stairs, and another on the rocks above the beach. All were elderly, frail. The first one was the Mother Superior from the earlier story, Mother Angelica. Sad, but nothing supernatural.

"Looks like nuns were dying left and right," I said. "No wonder they wanted to close the place. It was depopulating." I thought back to Vaughn's talk of pranks, the bizarre bonfires. "This must be where the Halloween rituals come from, so many deaths. No wonder the kids think the place is haunted. Winterbay Abbey is tragedy central."

"It *is* haunted," Emily said. "It has to be. That nun, Pamela Mayo, is haunting the abbey."

I swallowed. "We don't have real evidence of that, if there even is such a thing as real evidence of a ghost."

"Of course we do," Emily said. "You just said she was the girl you saw drown. That's why the police found nothing. You saw a ghost. I bet those teenagers have seen her too."

I shook my head. "Her body probably washed out to sea," I said. "It will turn up."

Emily sighed as if humoring a disbelieving child. She held up her good hand and ticked off her fingers. "The drawing of the abbey, the girl in the window, the bells, the tower room, the cradle, rattle, the figure in the shadow. She's trying to contact you, tell you something."

"No." I shook my head again. "There's another, *real* explanation. There has to be." Although right at that moment, I couldn't think of one.

"Will," Emily said. "Stop being so blind. You saw her reenact her death." She stopped and looked back at the screen, her gaze suddenly fixed and unmoving, eyes glassy. With her injured hand, she reached down and grabbed her knitting bag, pulling it into her lap where she slipped her hand inside, hiding it from view. After another moment, she said, "It's up to us to save her."

"Save her? What do you mean? She's already dead," I said.

Emily shook her head. "She might be dead, but she's not resting in peace. If she was, she wouldn't be haunting the beach, or you," Emily said. "It only makes sense. She wants your help. That's why you saw her."

The jump in Emily's logic sounded ridiculous. How could she have come to a conclusion so far-fetched?

"Look, you've been chosen for a very special job," she said.

"Well, I don't want it."

Emily's eyes never left the photo of Pamela on the monitor. "Of course you do. It's an honor to ease the pain of the dead. I wish she'd chosen me."

"Okay, Em," I said, putting my hand on her shoulder and turning her toward me. "Let's just focus on saving ourselves from financial ruin, okay? We don't need to be helping anyone but ourselves right now. We came here to answer some questions and clear my mind of worry, not go ghost hunting."

"She needs us," Emily whispered. "She's suffering." Emily turned her head back. Her gaze was locked on the computer, her body rigid, her right hand buried in her bag.

I took her other hand. "Hey, I think we need to go. We can look at this a little bit later. This has been without a doubt the worst day of my life," I said, standing up.

"No, I'm staying here to find out more," she said, sharply.

I glanced around. A librarian was staring at us as she cataloged magazines.

"Emily, come on. It's time to go," I said, pulling her shoulders back.

She swiveled in her chair, facing me. "See, this is exactly what I'm talking about. Why can't you just be supportive for once in my life?!" Her shout echoed through the library.

My jaw fell. Emily never yelled like that. *Ever.* I tried to help her up from her chair, but she swatted my hand away.

The male librarian got up from his seat and headed toward us.

"Excuse me, but I'm going to have to ask you to either quiet down or leave," he said, glancing first at me and then at Emily.

Dumbfounded, I tried to think of something to say. "Uh, I'm really sorry. I think my wife hasn't been…feeling well," I said, linking my arm in Emily's.

"I'm fine," Emily said. She dropped my arm again and stormed toward the front entrance.

I threw the librarian a sheepish look and ran after her.

I followed Emily back to the hotel. She pushed ahead of me every time I caught up. It was a short walk, and I'd have to return to pick up the car later. Silence loomed between us. I wanted to say a thousand things to comfort her, apologize, and brainstorm solutions, but I didn't think she wanted to hear any of them now. In any case, I usually said something stupid and didn't want to make the situation any worse. Maybe we actually needed to see a marriage counselor.

I understood why she was resentful. The hand injury had changed her life unalterably, and I'd walked away unscathed. Yet it made me angry that she'd didn't seem to understand I lived with the guilt and pain of that day every day.

I really wondered if she would ever be able to truly forgive me. Not only for the accident, but also for my reaction when she told me she was pregnant.

This nonsense of Pamela's ghost was only making everything worse, and I couldn't figure out why Emily was so hell-bent on us helping Pamela.

When we got back to the room, I turned on the gas fire, put a blanket over her, and heated some water for tea, all of which she accepted without comment. When the coffee pot beeped that it had finished heating, I poured the water into a mug with a bag of Earl Gray and handed it to Emily.

She stared up at me. "She really is a ghost."

"Yeah, so you keep saying," I said, a slight edge to my tone.

"I just wish I knew why she chose you," Emily said, staring into her mug.

I let out a long breath. "I don't want to talk about it anymore, Em." I plopped onto the bed and looked down at the geometric pattern on the hideous orange carpet. "It's been a long, strange day. Ghosts or not, I'm just going to finish my conceptual drawings."

"Aren't you even a little bit curious?" Emily asked. She took a sip and winced, spilling some of the tea on her bad hand. She barely flinched, with much of her sensitivity gone.

"Sorry," I said. "That's still pretty hot."

Emily pulled the blanket closer and blew on the tea. She peered over the edge of the cup. "Well? Aren't you curious?" she said again.

"I don't know. A little maybe, but I don't want to get involved," I said, hoping we were done with this conversation.

She glared at me. "Not all the spirits of the dead stay behind, otherwise they'd be everywhere all the time. But the ones who do, they aren't resting. Maybe we both can send her on to a more peaceful place."

"You say you can feel your dad watching over you," I said. "But he's resting in peace, isn't he?"

Her eyes darted at me. "That's different. He's not haunting me. My dad is watching from heaven."

"And this is different?"

"Of course. This ghost, Pamela, is somehow stuck here on earth, repeating her death over and over. She needs to be released from her pain. We need to release her."

"Will you just *please* stop?" I snapped, louder than I wanted. This conversation was becoming repetitive. "I need to focus on the task ahead. Our future depends on it, and I don't want to screw things up because I'm off chasing after ghosts."

She continued her hard stare.

What was going on with her? She wanted me to do these new jobs Ted and James had offered. So why wouldn't she lay off? Hadn't we argued *enough* today?

"I'm going for a walk," she said, coolly. She tossed her blanket aside and grabbed her pea coat.

"A walk? *Now*? You can't just go out at night in the cold," I said.

"Stop trying to control me." Her face was a mask of sternness again.

"Emily, we need to stop fighting. Please. I'm not trying to control you. I just care about you, and I'm sorry about everything today. I'm on edge and need some sleep. How about we look into this more by talking to some other people in town? There's a guy I met the other night named Martin. I think he may know some things about the abbey. How about I ask him some questions?"

Emily made it halfway to the door. She stopped but still didn't turn to face me.

I walked over to her, and put my arm around her. "Please," I said, trying to ease off her jacket.

Her shoulder muscles tensed as I touched her; then they relaxed a bit as she let out a sigh.

"Okay, thank you. All I want are some answers," she said, this time more calmly. "I think we need to speak with the police too. I think Vaughn knows more than he's saying."

I blinked. This was becoming a full-scale investigation. I opened my mouth to protest and then thought better of it. If I didn't give in to Emily, this really would be an all-out war.

"And, yeah, I do want you to find out more information through that Martin person," she added.

"Let me get some work done over the next couple of days, and then we'll look into it."

She shifted her stance. "Okay, thank you. I appreciate it," she said.

I guided her back to the chair and wrapped the blanket around her again. Quickly I turned on the TV, desperate for some distraction. After I put the remote down, I rested my head against the headboard as we watched the local news.

I reached into my pocket and took out my bottle of Tylenol. I swallowed two, all the while brainstorming how I was going to save my marriage, do my job, and not become entangled in the abbey and its supernatural vortex.

CHAPTER FIFTEEN

My sleep was interrupted by more nightmares seeping to the surface. Dreams of cradles rocking on their own coupled with bird attacks had me tossing and turning all night.

Morning came too soon. I dreaded the thought of returning to the abbey, especially alone. Emily and I ate a quick breakfast at another cafe down the street from the hotel, and I took her back to the inn. She curled up with her knitting.

"What's that you're making?" I asked. "Another sweater?"

She shook her head. "I'm not quite sure yet. We'll see."

I nodded, glad she was at least going to be productive, and that it would keep her from wanting to delve into the spirit world…for the moment.

Emily smiled. Genuine warmth exuded from her expression.

She seemed a lot better than yesterday. Maybe last night's reaction at the library was just a result of our fight in the car. We were both emotionally raw right now.

Maybe she was also happier because I'd promised I would try to find out information about the abbey's history. Although, I only planned to do the bare minimum—if anything at all.

I didn't have time to track down Martin. If I happened to see him on the street, I'd ask him a question or two.

Despite her improved attitude, it was still apparent that Emily and I couldn't stay in Winterbay. I had a feeling this ghost story would drive a further wedge between us. I needed to convince Ted and James I could work from home. If I could get the details I needed to complete my schematic designs and finish the pre-design work, have it accepted, and then tell them that Emily needed to fly home to see her doctor or something, we'd have no reason to remain here any longer. The ghost's problems would have to wait for the next unsuspecting dupe who happened to see her.

When I kissed Emily goodbye, she didn't seem overly concerned about me going back to the abbey by myself. Last night she'd acted more interested in helping a ghost than in any danger the situation might pose to me. In all honesty, the thought of being at the abbey terrified me.

I walked back to the library to get the car and drove to the abbey.

The wound on my forehead began to ache again as I made my way over the small bridge outside the abbey. I tried to think of the job ahead and not Pamela. I told myself she was not a ghost, and there was no ghost at all. That didn't stop the shivering that coursed through me. The closer I got to the abbey, the more my body objected.

A flash of the young nun raided my thoughts. *Pamela Mayo*. Her expression had been so angry, so accusing. Hate-filled enough that recalling her now frightened me more than ever.

I put my hand on the passenger seat, thinking of Emily. Shaking my head, I replaced the image of Pamela with one of Emily, smiling, happy, and holding our twins in her arms.

Immediately, a thin branch of warmth spread through my chest, and some of the anxiety ebbed. I needed to make this daydream a reality, to see Emily happy again. We had to find joy…to find it with our new family. If I could just hold onto this vision of Emily, maybe it would give me enough strength for today.

I slowed and made my way down the muddy road toward the convent.

I pulled up in front. The drive was empty.

Looming on the horizon, heavy clouds promised more rain. The chill heralded that it would be freezing rain.

After sitting in the car for another minute trying to convince myself to get out, I opened the trunk and pulled out my computer bag. I had a lot of work to do. I needed detailed laser scans of the entire building to move forward with the design, generate renderings, and make working from Seattle just as easy as being here. But it was going to take some time to finish.

I stood at the front entrance beneath the arch.

After summoning what courage I had, I flipped on my flashlight and walked up the main stairs, figuring I'd work my way from top to bottom. I had to scan every room, including a climb up into the tower with the creepy cradle.

Setting the equipment up, leveling the laser, and starting the scan wasn't easy in the dim light. I had better lights, but without a power source they were of no use.

The clouds had darkened by the time I finished. Thankfully nothing out of the ordinary had happened. No bells. No toys.

No rocking cradles. No shadowy figures looming in the corner. No ghosts.

As the final scan finished its run, I saved all the work on my computer and got ready to head downstairs. The last rooms on my tour were in the basement.

I walked along the narrow entry hall in search of the stairs to the bottom level. The warped, wooden floor must have been flooded at one time, probably a broken pipe. The texture felt like walking across the rocks on the beach, uneven and lumpy.

I still needed to figure out the building's mechanical systems to see what might be saved and what would need to be replaced. I'd let the engineers figure out what energy-efficient system they wanted. The plumbing wasn't extensive enough for all the rooms I planned, and the radiators had all looked rusted beyond rescue. Nor was there any way the wiring was up to code.

I tried several doors that led to closets long emptied of their contents. The fourth one creaked on its corroded hinges and stuck halfway open. The floorboards had swollen right in front of it, and no amount of straining on my part would get it to move any further. I stuck my head through the narrow opening and peered down into the dark. Wooden steps as uneven as the floor headed downward, cut off by a turn in the stairs.

The smell, a pungent mix of musty dampness and a sour reek, gagged me like a finger down my throat. I put my left sleeve over my mouth and leaned into the doorway.

Moving the light back and forth, I tried to see further into the depths without actually taking a step. A child-sized slab of mold stained the wall, the source of the stench and yet another remodel problem.

After taking a deep breath, I pushed through the stuck door and inched down the stairs to look for the boiler room.

The basement was in far worse shape than I'd imagined. As I got to the bottom of the stairs, my foot caught on something, and I pitched head-first into a pile of trash. Although the soggy mess broke my fall, the smell of the mold and rot made my head spin and renewed my headache. My flashlight skittered away, spinning along the floor in a twirl of light, and my computer bag hit the floor with a thud.

I retrieved both, hoping the bag's padding prevented any damage. I continued deeper into the basement. It didn't take long for me to realize I wasn't going to get much done with the small amount of illumination the flashlight provided. I'd never be able to inspect or do scans thoroughly enough to draw up plans. I'd probably have to bring in a small generator for lights and a respirator in case there were more fungal toxins.

I needed to check for the location of the plumbing stacks and furnace. I wandered down a narrow hall with pipes running over my head. One had a jagged hole. I followed the piping and soon found a rusted metal door marked *Boiler Room*. Unlike the door above, this one gave way with a slight push and a creak of rusted hinges. The old oil boiler sat tired and unused in a large mechanical room.

I stared at the maze of pipes shooting out of the boiler like a steampunk octopus, twisting tentacles running off to who knew where. They'd all have to be ripped out. Too bad. Old-fashioned radiators always provided a comfy ambiance, and if they actually functioned, plenty of warmth as well. Maybe some could be saved for a few special rooms.

I swept the light over the rest of the room, giving it a good once-over. A rat scurried away, jolting me, a reminder of that mysterious swarm of birds. I still couldn't figure out where they'd gone or how they'd left so little trace of their visit.

One more mystery I didn't need to think about right now.

After maybe ten minutes of peering at rusted machinery, I'd had enough. I picked up my computer bag. Back in the hall, outside the boiler room, I noticed a door, slightly ajar. Giving it a good push with my foot, I found myself looking into a storage room filled with shelf after shelf of file boxes piled up to the ceiling. I walked inside to take a closer look. Unlike the trash in the rest of the basement, these boxes hadn't been touched by water. Apart from years of accumulated dust, they weren't rotten at all.

Out of curiosity, I pointed my light at the nearest box. It was unlabeled, so I pulled the lid off and saw a collection of folders stuffed full of papers. This room had to be where all the abbey's records were kept. Why they'd been left behind, I couldn't imagine. I'd think the Catholic Church would have done a better job keeping track of old files.

I exhaled in exhaustion. Looking back down at the shelves of boxes, I thought about Emily pressuring me to find out about the abbey's history. Maybe this random collection of old records would reveal something so she and I wouldn't have to get more involved with the police, or Martin.

Knowing my luck, it was probably just old accounting documents or bills for incense.

I pulled out the first folder that touched my hand. I was right. The front was marked, EXPENDITURES 1919.

I looked at a few more boxes. None contained anything of the remotest interest.

I slid the last box back onto the shelf, and something thudded to the floor on the other side. Walking around to see what had happened, I found I'd knocked another box on the floor.

I stooped over and tried to shove the spilled papers back into the box. My eye caught a label on one folder: ADOPTIONS, 1915-1920.

I flipped through more folders. All were adoption files organized in five-year increments.

Strange. Had the abbey been doubling as an orphanage?

That would explain the cradle.

Maybe I had gotten lucky.

I shined my flashlight on another folder marked, ADOPTIONS 1960-1965. The top sheet of the first file contained only a few lines: child's name, sex, date of birth, date of adoption, and the mother's name. No listing of fathers.

The first sheet was marked with the name Wilma Foster. Baby's name Elizabeth. Adopted July 23, 1960. Mother deceased, July 26, 1960.

Next was a girl named Barbara Cholinski, baby boy, Stephen. Adopted December 5, 1963. Mother deceased December 8, 1963. In a third folder, date of birth March 7, 1965, child's sex male, adoption on March 8, 1964. The mother's name: Helen Kelly. Deceased March 10, 1964. Weird. All three mothers died within days of their babies' adoptions.

The last name I recognized from the library search. Helen Kelly had drowned like Pamela. Odd. *Kelly had been a nun.*

I scratched my head. A nun with a baby? *I guess there were more unheard-of things in the world.* But there had been no mention of a child in the newspaper article at the library.

I flipped through one folder after another of girls giving up their newborns for adoption, two dozen at least, the last adoption and death occurring just two months before the abbey was finally closed in 1969.

Some, like Wilma, Barbara, Helen, and a couple other girls—including the one from 1969—had died shortly after giving birth. For the rest, nineteen of them, no information. Neither was the cause of death listed for the five who had died. The newspaper had only reported Helen Kelly's drowning.

Had the girls, except for Helen, died from childbirth complications? I doubted the abbey was equipped with the best medical equipment and resources of the day. That would explain why the babies would need to be adopted. Except that some of the mothers appeared to have died after the adoptions were finalized.

Why had these women been at Winterbay Abbey when they gave birth, and why had those five died so shortly after?

One thing was for sure, there had been babies here.

A lump grew in my throat as I thought of all the misery and sadness here. The files I'd looked at covered just the 1960s. How many other girls had given away their babies and even died here before then? And all of it kept quiet—not a word in the news of the abbey being home to a possible institutionalized tragedy.

As I stared at the papers, for perhaps the first time, I finally felt a connection, deep inside, to my own children. The names on the files began to form a blank wall of fear. A fear of losing Emily and being separated from our children. I closed my eyes and drew up Emily's face, her smile.

After a deep breath, I looked back at the box of folders. I knew more about the abbey now, but what of Pamela? How did she connect to all of this? Did she have a file in here too?

I put Helen's paper down and shuffled through the rest of the folders. There was no file for Pamela. Why should there be? She was a nun, like Helen, but there was no reason to believe she'd been pregnant, too.

Her death had been reported in the paper, unlike most of the others. Why hadn't they made the news? Perhaps women dying after childbirth wasn't considered news, or perhaps the abbey hadn't wanted their deaths reported. That was more sinister. Though after seeing that tower room, my mind ran to ominous places.

Helen had died the same way as Pamela, drowned, and perhaps discovered by someone outside the abbey, making it impossible to cover up. That seemed like a logical explanation, if leaning toward the criminal.

I thought back to my conversation with Emily. She'd mentioned that ghosts stay behind when they have unfinished business.

What was Pamela's?

Had she known what was going on here with these other women and been killed for it?

I shook my head. I was falling down a rabbit hole.

I'd had enough.

Just then, a breeze sprang up, tracing down the back of my neck like a cold finger. That strange overflow of loneliness followed. It was the same one I'd felt in the tower room, as though the leaking pipes had flooded the basement with a sadness of loss. Except this time, I felt no fear, rather an anger, red hot and burning. Anger for being left alone and abandoned. No, not abandoned. *Betrayed*?

The emotions felt like someone else's being imposed on me.

The anger, the sheer hatred I felt burning behind my eyes, took hold of me. It boiled up from my stomach and shot through me like a white-hot flame. I threw the folders down and screamed at the top of my lungs. Lashing out, I kicked the boxes over, sending their contents spilling onto the dust-covered floor.

"Damn you all!"

My shouts echoed off the concrete walls, filling the dark with a hatred so vile and pure it actually made me queasy.

Then just as quickly, the burning emotion and the breeze passed. Before I could even figure out why I was so overwhelmed, I stood cold and shaking in the dank hole under the abandoned building. I slumped against the nearest wall, shivering uncontrollably, hugging myself hard enough to leave fingerprints on my arms. I felt wet and freezing, almost as badly as when I'd raced into the surf to save Pamela.

What was going on? I couldn't stop shaking.

After another minute, I regained my composure. I needed to get out of here.

I glanced around the room. The loneliness had gone, and the papers I'd attacked lay strewn on the floor. I picked up the folder with Wilma, Barbara, and Helen's files again. I wanted to show it to Emily. Hopefully this would satisfy her need for more information about the abbey, at least for a little while.

I made my way back upstairs, crossing my fingers that whatever overtook me would stay in the basement.

I dashed down the front steps to my car. Before I got in, a sharp noise echoed from the woods. My body tensed. A gust of wind swayed the trees, making their loose branches squeak. Squinting in the cloudy grayness, I spotted a grouping of stones near the grove. Sitting about fifty yards back from the beach, just inside the forested tree line, were several rows of gray headstones—the abbey's cemetery. I'd noticed it when I first arrived but had put it out of my mind. The gravestones leaned at odd angles, a wind and weather-ravaged collection of stone reminders of life. Perhaps there were more answers here.

I put the adoption folder on the front seat and trudged toward the cemetery, stopping near the base of a large pine at the entrance. Engraved on the tree was the letter P with a heart around it. I ran my fingers over the initial. Immediately, an image of my first day here played in my head. *The writing on the wall.* "P, I love you. Forgive me." That letter P had also had a heart encircling it.

"Pamela?" I whispered.

Walking into the tightly packed cemetery, I passed beneath an iron arch with Winterbay etched into a sign. Beneath were the words of Psalm 23: *Surely goodness and mercy shall follow me all the days of my life, and I will dwell in the house of the Lord forever.*

I brushed the moss away from the first headstone. The date was 1921. I moved on. Next was from the 1930s for a nun born before the Civil War. I checked a few more. All seemed to be for nuns, old ones. I spotted another from 1962, one I recognized from the newspaper. *Mother Angelica Murray. 1899-1962. I have fought the good fight; I have finished the race; I have kept the faith.* She certainly seemed sure of herself. Considering the history of this place, far too sure.

I moved to what looked like a newer portion, less overgrown, the headstones still standing upright. My blood began to race as I ran from stone to stone, cleaning away the dirt and lichens to reveal the inhabitants' identities. There they were—Wilma, Barbara, Helen, all the girls from the files.

Yet nothing of Pamela.

I looked at each grave again, sweeping away the dirt of decades. Pamela was not here.

Perhaps she had been sent home to her family.

I rubbed my hands together and wandered back out through the iron gate, still unsure of what to make of everything. Ten yards from the cemetery, I stopped. A lone marker buried beneath a jade-colored fern protruded from the ground. Pulling the wet plant aside and brushing away the soil and dead leaves, I saw: *Pamela Mayo—1943-1961.*

I'd found her. She was only 18.

Why was the grave here, outside the fence of the cemetery? Unless Emily was right.

The girl I'd seen was reenacting her death, and she'd headed straight into the surf.

Pamela was a suicide. That had to be why she was not in the main cemetery. The Church usually considered suicide a mortal sin, leaving victims unfit for burial in hallowed ground. But if she'd killed herself, any idea of her being murdered in a conspiracy to cover up deaths at the abbey was off-base.

A twig snapped. I jumped up and spun around as I heard a shuffling from behind. My body grew cold when I saw someone among the trees.

CHAPTER SIXTEEN

The figure stood in the shadows of the trees for a moment, then began to grow in size as it approached. An old man in a grease-stained yellow rain slicker stepped out of the dark and pointed a large flashlight at me.

Duncan.

"Excuse me, what are you doing here!?" I asked while trying to control the shaking in my voice.

He didn't answer, only continued to approach me. The look in his eyes was unsettling, filled with a cloudy anger. He put his hood up. "Go home, and take your fancy-pants developers with you," he said in his thick accent.

"That's not going to happen," I said. "Besides, I'm not the one spending millions on this building restoration."

"You'll get no more warnings," he said. He turned and strode off.

I followed him through the tall grass toward the beach. "Are you behind all those strange things that have been going on in the abbey? Like ringing the bell?" I called.

He stomped on without a word.

"Why are you here?" I shouted.

He waved his flashlight toward the lighthouse in reply to my question. Only the beam of its spinning light shone through the mist of the low-lying clouds. An icy wind whipped around us and the grass and trees.

"You were out at the lighthouse in this weather?" I asked, finally catching up to him. I pointed toward the warning light.

He made a hacking sound in his throat and then spat near his feet. "I check it from the beach. Make sure the light's still shining."

I shook my head. The light could be seen up and down the coast. There was no reason for him to be here to check.

"You've been following me," I said. "You were in that tower. You rang the bell."

He spat again. The corners of his eyebrows lowered like two seesaws on their downward slope. At first I'd seen him as angry or menacing, but now his look seemed more pained. "Like I said, this is no place for a hotel."

I sighed. "What do you mean?" I asked.

He glared at me with his gray eyes.

Raindrops began splattering on my head.

Duncan looked up. "You've seen things; you should know."

I nodded. "I *have* seen things, strange things. Too many. That's why I *need* to know. What's going on?"

He shifted his eyes toward the sea and paused, as if grappling with a difficult decision. "Not here," he said with a sigh. "My place. It's just a ways ahead up the beach. Let's walk."

I glanced in the direction he indicated. Was it really a good idea to go anywhere with this guy?

He must have noticed my hesitation. "You'll want to hear this," he said. "You saw the graves. What I have to tell you might save your life." He jerked his head toward the cemetery and breathed deeply.

My throat went dry, taking in what he was saying. I stared up into the sky. Thick clouds sailed across the vast expanse, releasing their burden of rain. I didn't know why, but deep down I feared he was right, that somehow my life was in danger.

After a moment, I nodded.

Duncan lumbered along, and I followed as we made our way up the rocky beach. A light surf frothed at the water's edge, beating the rocks with foam. The already dense fog thickened, and in the growing dark, I could barely see to step around the wet, slime-covered rocks. More than once, I slipped and stumbled.

Raindrops continued to pelt my head, multiplying in intensity. The cold struck so deeply I found myself wishing for the relative comfort of the dark, moldy basement of the abbey. It was getting so frigid that I felt snow would be our next pleasure. I should have offered to drive.

I glanced over at Duncan. He strode ahead, silent, sure-footed.

After a half-mile hike along the increasingly narrow beach, Duncan looked up toward the wooded slope above us and lifted his finger. "Up there."

He turned and began a slow ascent of a narrow, winding path through thick evergreens shrouded in mist. Like giant guardians, the trees watched us struggle up the moss-lined path. I imagined how beautiful this forest was in summertime. Now it was a cold, foggy gauntlet that closed in behind us. The trail wound back and forth. With each turn, I felt more cut off from home and comfort.

Duncan had chosen a dismal spot to live.

I skirted around a large tree, and the path widened a little. About 30 feet ahead, was a small cabin nestled between two large raised gardens and a wooden gate. Its siding was dark with a brilliant red door and trim. Ivy grew up a white trellis all the way to the house's chimney. The intricate, Gothic-looking woodwork was beautiful, a tiny Hansel and Gretel cottage in the woods.

I hoped I hadn't just followed the wicked witch home.

CHAPTER SEVENTEEN

Duncan walked ahead of me to the porch. As soon as the front door opened, a Saint Bernard came bounding toward me. I took a few steps back. The dog had the biggest head I'd ever seen.

It barked, the noise reverberating through the vast forest, making me wonder if I should turn and run.

"Gryffin, back!" Duncan yelled from inside.

The dog retreated into the house.

Still pensive, but shivering from the cold, I followed. The smell of wood smoke wafted toward me along with an aroma of seasoned cooking. Duncan was poking the fire in a wood-burning stove against the back wall. A small black-iron cauldron sat atop the burner.

Gryffin sat next to him, shifting his eyes back and forth between Duncan and me.

"He doesn't bite. Friendly as a lamb," he said. "Drools buckets, though."

Gryffin flopped down next to a rocking chair that had a fiddle resting on its upholstered seat.

I glanced around. The red tone of the cherry woodwork complemented the cottage's surprisingly warm atmosphere. Every nook was tidy, including the kitchen. A small brass teapot, copper pans on S-hooks above the wood stove, and a collection of antique copper soup ladles on the wall were the only appliances in sight.

There were no modern electronics. A bookshelf of leather-bound volumes and worn paperbacks sat in the corner next to a small upholstered couch. A painting hanging over the mantle in the living room caught my eye. It was a watercolor of a rustic fishing village clustered with brilliant red, blue, and navy 18th-century-looking houses. As I stared at the artwork, the slow tick-tock of two ornately carved cuckoo clocks echoed off the walls in the kitchen and living room.

If this was a witch's house, it was a nice one.

"Sit. I'll bring the food over," he said with a wave toward a small table with two chairs. "Need to eat. Don't want my blood sugar to get too low."

I hadn't planned on eating but wasn't one to turn down a meal.

Gryffin sat at my feet and put a paw on my thigh. I reached down and patted him. He came closer, nuzzling against my leg like a cat. *Gentle as a lamb, all right.*

Duncan put down two wooden bowls full of a thick soup. A sprinkling of bacon covered what looked like a hearty mixture of leeks, turnips, parsnips, and maybe lamb.

Duncan sat himself. "*Cawl*," he said as he pushed a bowl in front of me. "Mam's recipe."

"Thanks," I said, taking a bite. The stew wasn't at all bad, and I was glad for some warmth from the cold. "So, did you know Pamela?" I asked straight out.

He set down his spoon and wiped his mouth on his sleeve. "Yes. It all started with her."

"I figured as much," I said. "So there really is a ghost that haunts the abbey." I couldn't believe I was saying this out loud.

He nodded. "Then you *do* believe."

"Like I said, I've seen things."

He nodded and got up, bringing out butter, tea, and bread with dried fruit chunks baked inside the loaf.

Gryffin sat patiently, licking his slobbery lips.

"I used to live out at the lighthouse," Duncan said. "That was more than fifty years ago. It's automated now. Can't believe it. I had just turned 25 then. The lighthouse was quiet work, and I liked it. Never really much of a people person. I like being on my own. When I wasn't out on the rock, I'd help out around Winterbay Abbey, mowing the grass, keeping up the grounds. You know, odd jobs. The nuns were quiet too, and I liked that. On Sunday evenings they'd invite me in for a meal. They were strict. Mother Superior Angelica, especially. She seemed to take a liking to me, though. At least in the beginning. Not sure why."

"She was the nun who died falling down the stairs, right? I saw it in the paper."

"Yes," Duncan said. "I guess you've been doing some research. There were more nuns' deaths as well. The Church shut down Winterbay a few years later. All the sisters were elderly, and it was too expensive to keep the old place running."

"It was more than just expense and aging nuns that shut it down," I said. "*All* those deaths—nuns, those young girls. And all of it looks like it had been kept secret. I can't help but think that they were covering something up."

He cleared his throat. "Let me finish."

I nodded.

"Anyway, it was mid-summer when Pamela came to the nunnery, only a month or so after I'd first arrived. She was young, and I noticed her right off, quiet as a scared kitten, not looking at anyone for more than a quick glance. She was beautiful though. Her soft features and bright eyes kept me transfixed."

Duncan described a different look than I'd seen on the beach, or even in the newspaper photo.

He drank a gulp of his tea. "The novitiates, that's the new nuns, weren't allowed to speak with any employees, especially men. The older sisters did all the talking."

"Wait a minute," I said. "Just nuns? Weren't there any others there? Other girls?"

Duncan glared at me. "Yes, there was always at least one girl there who wasn't a nun. *Guests* they called them."

"Pregnant?"

He nodded. "That's how it was in those days. Unwed girls, sent off to nunneries, kept out of sight to avoid embarrassing their families. Went on all the time. We just accepted it. It was never talked about. The Church always kept it quiet too. Let the families avoid the shame, and because of their fear of speaking openly about sin, lest it cause more."

I took a sip of my tea. It burned with a hint of whiskey. The adoption files I'd found were beginning to make sense. "Do you remember any names of the 'guests'?"

"If you want to know about Pamela, you'll have to let me tell it my way," he said, his eyes narrowing.

I tipped my cup toward him.

"So," he went on with a sigh, "every now and then I'd sneak a peek down the table at Pamela silently staring at her plate.

Once or twice I caught her looking and winked at her to say hello, as we couldn't speak. She turned red and looked away, I'm sure frightened of being caught by the Mother Superior. Her punishments were severe. There were rumors about what that woman subjected the nuns to. Beatings, confinement. Hours, days on end without food, kneeling on a cold stone floor in penance, praying for forgiveness—and worse. That woman thought she could literally put the fear of God in people, that and she seemed to think that through torture she could cleanse women of their sins."

I took another swig of my tea. Those punishments seemed fitting, coming from a woman whose tombstone bragged that she'd "fought the good fight." Had she been the one who kept so many deaths and adoptions a secret? But she'd died less than a year after Pamela and before some of the other girls.

Duncan went on. "From those few glances, I could tell Pamela felt as out of place as I did, and that I had a friend. Every Sunday we'd sit at the same table with some of the other nuns and employees, and sometimes *guests*.

"I loved seeing Pamela smile. Two weeks after we first met, I baked some Welsh cakes with currants and brought them to her to serve at our table. I'll never forget how delighted she looked when I handed her the basket, and she lifted the cloth. After dinner when everyone was eating dessert, some of the powdered sugar from the cakes dusted Pamela's nose. I kept signaling her to wipe it off. She didn't quite know what I meant until finally, I whispered it to her. She immediately blushed and took out her handkerchief. Finally, she did laugh, still red in the face. Laughing was forbidden, and she tried to keep as quiet as she could, but it made me chuckle too. It was hard to control ourselves. Pamela kept coughing to cover up her giddiness. Looking back, that was the first time I'd laughed and felt joy since moving to Maine. I never wanted the moment to end.

"After that night, Pamela and I would volunteer to clean up after dinner just to spend more time together. We were never alone, and always on opposite sides of the room, but I still relished that time.

"Pamela took her vows seriously and followed the abbey's rules to the letter, or so I thought. After about a month or so of our cleaning after meals, she began to sing a little bit to herself. Soft, far away, not-of-this-world humming. I focused on every song, trying to recognize the melodies. Then, to my utter shock, she said 'hello' to me when no one else was looking. It was in a hushed whisper. I would have missed it if I'd not been straining to hear her every sound. When I first heard her voice, I was nearly hypnotized by her quiet lilt. I longed to learn everything about her.

"Finally one night in the kitchen during a warm summer rainstorm, Pamela started talking in a quickened, hushed tone. I remember glancing around, hoping no one had heard. As much as I wanted to converse with her, I always worried she would get into trouble. She told me all about her childhood, living as an orphan after her parents had both died in a car accident, and her love for knitting and singing. I was enthralled. Before we parted, she sang a song for me, of angels and her faith. I told her I played the fiddle. She said she hoped to hear me one day.

"After that, Pamela and I talked whenever the other sisters weren't looking, which wasn't always easy. Sometimes after meals, or over a shrub in the garden. I spent the rest of my week out on the rock, tending the light and thinking about that lovely voice, those emerald eyes of hers, and songs I could accompany her with on my fiddle."

I glanced at his well-used instrument sitting on the corner chair.

"I loved Pamela since that first night. But she was a nun…who was I to interfere with God's plan for her life? And even if she did have feelings for me, which seemed clear from her glances, the way we spoke, and how she lingered during clean-ups, I was just getting my start in America. I barely made enough money to support myself, let alone a wife.

"I tried to forget my desires, forget her longing looks. It wasn't easy to put those green eyes out of my head, not when they're the first thing I thought of in the morning and the last thing at night."

I thought of Pamela's eyes as well, again, just not in the same way as Duncan.

"After hemming and hawing for months," he went on, "I finally wrote her a letter, telling her how I felt. I snuck it past Mother Superior Angelica's ever-watchful eye." He stopped and looked away, his voice thickening. "It was a selfish thing to do." He stood up and his legs wobbled. Duncan put a hand on the wall to balance himself.

Gryffin whined.

"Are you okay?"

"Fine," he said with a wave of his hand. He cleared his throat. "I was nervous to see her the next Sunday night. I came into the dining hall, sweating. When I glanced at our special table, she wasn't there. I asked one of the other nuns where she was. She told me that Pamela was fasting and would not be coming down to dinner. I feared we'd been found out, but the Mother Superior paid me no mind."

I put my cup down.

Duncan remained standing and swallowed the rest of his tea. "I feared the worst, that she was hiding from me, and I'd never see her again."

Gryffin came over and put his head in my lap. I scratched his neck, not breaking my gaze from Duncan.

Duncan walked to the stove. He looked agitated, his hands flitting over the teapot. After pouring himself a shot of whiskey, he returned to the table. He drew in a long breath. "You'll have to excuse me. I've never told anyone all this before."

I nodded, unsure of what to say. The worst of this story was yet to come, and I still had no idea what the hell this all had to do with my life being in danger.

"About a week after that Sunday dinner, I was here. This is where I stayed when not on duty at the lighthouse. My boss, who owned the house at the time, was out tending the lighthouse. I heard a knock and thinking it was my employer, I quickly opened the door. Instead, Pamela stood in front of me, her eyes bloodshot from crying.

"'I love you, too,' she'd said, putting her arms around me. 'I do, but I can't. I've made a commitment to God. I have prayed for guidance, and I'm convinced that getting married is not something I can do. The Church and the Lord truly are my calling. Yet I thought I'd never feel for a man in this way.'"

Duncan focused out the window, a thousand-yard stare.

"I saw how distraught and conflicted she was and guilt tore at me for having interfered in her life and causing her pain. Pamela deserved happiness. I told her I'd take her back to the abbey. She refused, saying she was too upset and didn't want to return until she was more put together. As a fog rolled in, it was too easy to agree with her. I started a fire, picked up my fiddle, and started playing 'Amazing Grace.' Pamela immediately began to sing."

Duncan's voice grew quiet, almost a whisper.

"The song had calmed her, and she began to smile. When it was over, she hugged me, and that embrace turned into a kiss. Before I knew it…" Duncan put his hand over his eyes.

I looked down at Gryffin to avoid staring at Duncan's pained face.

"I, I…" Duncan trailed off. He got up and walked into the kitchen. As he poured more liquor, his hands shook. He sat down and drank without offering me any.

"It's okay," I said lamely.

"No. No it's not!" he said, slamming his cup on the table. "We lost control of ourselves."

Gryffin hid behind the couch.

I scratched my neck, wondering if I should hide Duncan's bottle of whiskey, or get a drink for myself.

"It was more than a month until I heard from her again. I thought she was avoiding me in shame. She wrote me a letter. Said she knew her body was changing straightaway, but asked me not to try to see her. I feared what Mother Angelica might do to her. I never knew how much Pamela suffered until it was too late. All I knew was I wanted to run there and take her away to a place where we could be together. Instead, I did as she asked, even though I began to fear that Pamela would stay at the abbey and quietly give up the child for adoption."

"Like the other girls," I said. "Were they subjected to those same punishments from Mother Angelica?"

Duncan's face fell. "Of course they were. Times were different back then. Like I said, nunneries were always places for shamed families to send their pregnant daughters, hidden from the judgment of others. You should hear the awful convent tales out of Ireland—where Mother Angelica was from. The girls were sent to those places to be *disciplined* for their sins."

My stomach dropped at the thought. So little compassion for those women and their circumstances. I'd seen news from Ireland about abuses in the Church before but had never given it much thought.

This entire story was beginning to crystalize now. Except, who was the real villain here? Mother Superior Angelica, the ever-so-certain Irish nun? Perhaps Emily was right about Pamela having unfinished business. Had she returned to haunt Mother Angelica? If that were true, Pamela's purpose had been fulfilled, hadn't it? Angelica was dead. So why was Pamela still here? Why hadn't she passed on?

Duncan walked to a small locked cabinet. From under his shirt, he pulled out a key hanging around his neck. Gently, he unlocked the case, reached in, and took out a small silver box. Lifting the lid, he retrieved a gold necklace with a cross pendant, and two folded pieces of paper. He pressed the pages to his lips and came back to the table.

"This is the only thing I have she wrote for me," he said. He stared at the necklace, which I could only guess had belonged to Pamela. Finally, after what seemed a full minute, he unfolded the papers and handed them to me:

Dearest Duncan,

Please forgive the delay in this note. It was not easy to write. I'm sorry I did not speak to you since I first told you of my condition. I had to be alone to think everything over.

Although I care for you very much—no, I love you—I have pledged my life and my soul to God and to do His service here on earth, to be guided by His Angels. I have prayed night and day that the Lord forgive me my sins and accept my service. But service to the Lord requires sacrifices. And I'm afraid my sacrifice is that I must never see you again. If I do, I fear I would waver in my decision and be too tempted to accept you.

Good-bye and God-Bless. May you walk with the Angels.

Pamela

Underneath Pamela's letter was an adoption document like the ones I'd seen at the abbey. The paper read: born January 14, 1961, male, adopted January 27, 1961. The mother's name: Pamela Mayo. Deceased.

It had only taken two weeks from having her child until the boy had been adopted. Three days later she was dead, drowned. I'd witnessed the scene all over again on the beach.

I glanced again at the letter. If Emily had sent me something like this, I can't imagine what I would do.

"I wanted to strangle myself when I read her words," Duncan said. "I looked every Sunday for her. She never came down. All was kept quiet."

A low, sinking heaviness developed in my chest. "I saw that tower cell. It was so small, barely enough room to pace. Did they lock her in there as penance?"

Duncan let out a low moan, pain-filled and woeful. "I…if I had known…" he choked off a sob.

I folded the papers and handed them back to him. "Was that room where they sent all those pregnant girls?"

"I suppose, although I don't really know," he said, his voice nearly a wail. "Mother Angelica locked Pamela in there. Alone. I didn't know about the room until much later when I investigated the abbey after it was shut down."

An image of the small handprint on the tower room's hidden window sprang into my mind.

"There's something about all this that doesn't make sense. Why would Mother Angelica allow Pamela to stay and become a nun after knowing she was pregnant out of wedlock? Wouldn't that be an unforgivable sin?" I asked.

"That's just it. Mother Angelica thought she could *save* Pamela from her sins and her condition by way of harsh disciplinary means. She took it upon herself to be Pamela's savior." Duncan held his temples. "I…I can't believe how much I failed her," he said.

"What could you have done?" I asked, looking for some way to console him. But deep down, I knew he was right. "She'd taken her vows and promised to obey this Mother Angelica. You couldn't have known she was being imprisoned."

He slammed the table again. "I should have known! Should have had the guts to go in there and be a man. Demanded to see her. It was up to me to protect her."

I stared at the knots and patterns in the wooden tabletop. My stomach felt hollow, guilt burning inside me. I thought of my reaction to Emily when she first announced that she was pregnant. I'd freaked out and been an insensitive ass, wishing what Emily was saying wasn't true, and then mostly only caring about the logistics of the situation. *Would I have done more than Duncan in a similar situation to save the woman I love?*

Duncan tilted his head back and lifted his mug to his mouth.

I stared at him as he began to pour himself another. If he had any more, he'd be crying on the floor.

"Day after day went by with no word from her," Duncan continued. "I put up a calendar, crossing off every day 'til I got to nine months from *that day*. I planned to sneak into the abbey close to the due date and find her, beg her to come away with me. If she didn't want to come, I...at least I would've tried. I'd saved some money and borrowed a car so we could escape. Still I heard nothing. I couldn't risk poking around and asking questions, exposing myself too soon.

"I waited until my last X on the calendar, knowing it was a shot in the dark as far as when the baby would be born. I didn't want to wait any later. I was afraid that the new parents of our child would come and take the baby away. After lights-out, I made my way to the abbey. They were waiting for me: Mother Angelica and the police. I don't know how they knew I was coming. I assume Mother Angelica either guessed I was the father or maybe she'd tortured Pamela into revealing it. 'You leave this place forever,' she'd commanded. 'Pray God to forgive you your sins.' Then the police hauled me off for trespassing, and my last chance was gone."

"Did you tell them what was going on?" I asked.

"As much as I could, but I didn't know Pamela was imprisoned," Duncan said. A look of loss and despair clouded his eyes. "It wouldn't have mattered anyway. The police never listened to me. I think they knew what went on at the abbey. They never interfered. It was the Church, after all."

The Winterbay police not taking people seriously sounded all too familiar.

"The cops couldn't hold me, so I went to the lighthouse and holed up inside. I watched from the rock every day for any sign of her. The abbey remained locked up tight. Two weeks later, my life changed forever. There was a storm blowing in when I happened to spot Pamela through my binoculars. She had somehow slipped out of the abbey and was wandering on the beach. I raced down to the relief boat. Once I'd cleared the rock, I headed toward the landing up the way from the abbey, hoping she'd see me and meet me there.

"Swells washed into the boat, and the current pushed me far up the shore. As I approached the landing, a large flock of seagulls flew over my head, squawking and crying. They circled so low I had to duck and swat at the damned things to drive them off. Never seen such a thing, before or since."

Duncan's story of the birds sounded like my own run-in with those winged rats.

"It almost seemed that the sea itself was set against me."

"Bay of Lost Souls," I mumbled.

"What's that?" Duncan said. "What did you say?"

I shook my head. "Something I heard in town, about Winterbay being cursed."

He nodded and covered his face. "I raced straight for the beach, not caring if I split the boat open on the rocks. I lost sight of her as I made my way toward shore and then found her later, floating face down in the water. I pulled her into my boat. She was already gone." He choked off a sob. "Those lovely green eyes, cold and staring. I'll never forget that as long as I live." He squeezed the gold cross in his hand.

I realized I'd been holding my breath despite knowing the awful end of the story.

"It was my fault. She'd seen me and was coming out into the water to meet me. I just know it." A sob escaped his lips. "Mother Angelica claimed Pamela drowned herself on purpose.

I won't believe it, not ever!" He finished by knocking over his whiskey bottle.

Gryffin whimpered.

I took the opportunity to take the bottle away. "Is that why she's not buried inside the cemetery?" I asked, sliding the bottle underneath the table. "Because they thought she was a suicide?"

"She didn't kill herself." Tears trailed down his face.

I sat back. Despite his protests, it seemed more than apparent that Pamela probably had.

CHAPTER EIGHTEEN

This tale of Duncan's—lost love, stolen children, Pamela's torture at the hands of a vindictive nun, and suicide—provided plenty of reasons why Pamela might still be haunting Winterbay Abbey. Her tragedy—indeed the misfortune of the abbey itself and all those other "wayward" girls—was greater than I'd imagined. But what was I supposed to do about it? What did Pamela want, if anything, from me? And why did Duncan think my life was in danger?

These realizations elevated my anxiety to a new level. All I wanted was to be rid of Winterbay, escape from this town with all its tragic secrets.

"I'm sorry for your loss, truly. But could you please tell me what all this has to do with me?" I asked.

Duncan sat hunched over with his head on the table. He snapped his head up and glared at me, his eyes hot. "It was Mother Angelica. She drove her mad, drove Pamela to her death. She hated Pamela, wanted her to suffer."

Age-old hatred flamed in his eyes.

"Why?" I asked. "From what you've said, she was a stern woman, hard and cold, and she did some terrible things as

Mother Superior. But why would she have especially hated Pamela? It sounds like she treated her like all the other girls. And why would all of this lead to Pamela haunting the abbey if Mother Angelica was already dead?"

Duncan's held his head. "What?! Haven't you been listening? *Pamela*'s not haunting the abbey!"

"What do you mean?" I asked. "I saw her ghost on the beach. I know it was Pamela. It was the girl from the newspaper photo."

Duncan shook his head harder. "No! You've been fooled. Like I was at first. I thought Pamela's ghost had returned after I'd heard some of the strange rumors of the ghost. But if she had, she'd have come to me, not drowned all those girls." His voice lowered to a whisper. "I've never seen Pamela's ghost." Then, in a near shout, he pointed his finger at me. "*Mother Angelica* haunts the abbey."

I stared at him. How in the world had we taken this turn? He thought Angelica was the ghost and drowned some of the girls? "I don't understand," I said. "That makes no sense."

"Mother Angelica was a vicious, hateful bitch," Duncan said. "Her malevolence has continued beyond her death." Duncan cleared his throat. "She also believed in demons. Pamela was followed by angels."

"Followed by angels?" I asked.

"Pamela had a special connection with them, ever since she was a small girl, at the orphanage she grew up in. Used to talk to them. They guided her, gave her advice. At times, they were her only friends. That's why she was becoming a nun."

This story was starting to go off the deep end. Duncan was clearly drunk now. I slid my chair back, thinking it was time to leave.

"Sit down!" he yelled.

"Look, I've listened to this whole story. You've even got me believing in ghosts. But angels too? And you still haven't answered my question about what all this has to do with my life being in danger," I said, pointing at him.

Duncan waved a drunken hand at me. "Go on, get out!" he snapped. "I knew you wouldn't believe. You're like all the rest. I told people the same thing. Mother Angelica hating Pamela for her angels, jealous to the point of murder. That's the truth. The idea that Pamela could talk to angels drove Mother Angelica mad. She told Pamela they were demons, not angels. Pamela getting pregnant was the work of those demons, and Mother Angelica sent her to her death, torturing her to drive them out."

I sat there, gaping, not knowing what to believe. "You said Angelica killed the other girls too," I said. "By driving out their demons as well?"

Duncan nodded. "She tortured them all for their sins, same as Pamela. All the pregnant girls. And they all died the same way as Pamela, drowned."

I thought back to the newspaper records. There had been a death shortly before Pamela, perhaps more. I hadn't looked at the records for the previous decade. Did Angelica really cause those deaths?

"Drownings?" I asked. "The paper only mentioned one."

"They were all found on the beach. Mother Angelica covered that up."

"How do you know?"

"I know," he said.

"Why didn't anyone notice so many girls were dying?"

"They didn't all die, only a few, and like I said, it was covered up. It was easy enough to say they had died in childbirth. No one questioned the church back then."

"Not even parents?" I asked, not believing what I was hearing.

Duncan shook his head. "The girls were all like Pamela—orphans, or abandoned by shamefaced parents. Pamela was different, though." Duncan jumped up, unsteady on his legs, and staggered back to the cupboard where he'd retrieved Pamela's letter. He pulled a small book out of the same silver box and held it up. "Read this."

"What is that?" I asked.

"Pamela…" he choked, "Pamela's diary. I found it in a space beneath a loose floorboard, up in the tower," Duncan said. "Read what she says about Angelica, about how she twisted her mind."

As he handed me the book, a memory of the floorboard I'd found in the tower room surfaced. I'd shined my flashlight in the hole. It had been empty.

I glanced down at the red cover with the word *Diary* in scripted gold lettering on the front, just the sort of journal a young girl would have. I gently turned back the cover and saw *Pamela* written in fancy calligraphy on the inside front. "Okay," I said with a sigh. "But I still don't understand what this all has to do with me."

A blank stare hovered over his expression, as though he didn't recognize me for a split second.

"Duncan?"

"Just read it!" he snapped.

I frowned and opened the diary to the first entry:

Jan. 17, 1957

Dear Diary,

I'm fourteen years old today. The orphanage's headmistress reminded me again that I'll have no place to live in two more years. I miss my mom and dad. Why did God have to take them so early?

My angels say I have a destiny, but they haven't told me what it is yet.

June 29

The bright one came last night, Francine. I like to call her that, she's never told me her real name. She hovered over my bed, amazingly none of the other girls ever see her. She smiled and told me I must serve the Lord. That's what she always says mostly, but not how, or where or why, just that I must serve. I think I will ask Miss Blandeau, the headmistress. I won't tell her about my visions, but just to get an answer how best to serve here at the orphanage.

July 1

Miss Blandeau says I should become a nun, in fact she's surprised it took me this long to think of it. There's an abbey, Winterbay Abbey, in Maine, where she knows the Mother Superior and is sure I would be taken in and trained. There I would be able to help young girls and serve the Lord. I will ask Francine.

I hope they have lots of birds in Maine. We have them here, and I love to watch them. Sometimes I sit in class and just watch out the windows at the circling seagulls, calling and swirling over the yard.

July 14

It's been over two weeks since I last saw Francine.

I am afraid. Norman has come back. He's the grumpy angel. I call him Norman because he reminds me of the janitor who used to work here at St. Bridget's. Sometimes I still have nightmares about him. I was thankful one of the girls told Miss Blandeau about the blood they saw on my shirt before he was finally sent away. I was always so afraid. Angel Norman doesn't talk much, and he scares me sometimes. He stands in the dark corner of the bedroom here at night staring at me while I try to sleep. He usually only comes back when I have the dreams about my parents. I did ask him about becoming a nun, but he didn't answer. I must still ask Francine and trust her to protect me from Norman.

August 18

Sometimes I believe if I concentrate hard enough, I could really fly like the seagulls outside. Miss Blandeau chastises me for daydreaming, and I know Francine must want me to think more about the Lord than birds, but I believe that God made all creatures great and small and does not mind when I consider how beautiful His creation is. Their wings are so remarkable. They remind me of Francine's wings. Birds must be special sorts of angels sent from God. They are so free.

The entries stopped for a while, until Pamela was at Winterbay. I wasn't sure what to make of her "angels." They sounded almost like pets, or imaginary friends. Her fascination with birds was another uncomfortable reminder of my bird attack, and Duncan's tale of the day of Pamela's death.

July 1, 1959

Dear Diary,

My first day at Winterbay Abbey. Mother Superior Angelica is much like Miss Blandeau, only worse. She is very strict and stern, a scary little woman not more than 5 feet tall with iron gray hair and a gold tooth. She says that I must be open and honest, tell her the truth at all times, and keep nothing from her. I will try, but I am not sure about my angels. They've always been mine alone. I'll have to keep this diary hidden at least for now and hope that's not a sin.

There are a dozen nuns and two pregnant girls they call "guests." I've heard of girls who've gotten into trouble being sent to nunneries to avoid the embarrassment. Mother Angelica told me to stay away from the guests so their sinfulness doesn't corrupt me. I know what they've done is a sin, but I feel sorry and sad for them. They seem like nice girls and are my age. Can't they be forgiven?

Mother Superior Angelica showed me to a little dorm room, they call them all cells. It's not very comfy, and I'm so lonely. I miss St. Bridget's. Never thought I'd say that.

There are birds everywhere here, though. My room looks out toward the woods and not the sea, but I can watch them from the beach whenever I'm not busy studying or praying. Their wings are so beautiful and strong.

July 10, 1959

I feel so alone. The nuns here at Winterbay seem cold, like Mother Angelica. They're mostly older, some ancient, except for Sister Joanne, who's very nice and only a few years older than me, and I think I could be her friend. Mother Angelica is frightening. I've lost count of how many times she's lectured me about sin and doing penance. She carries a wooden pointer that she smacks in her hand while she speaks, or on my hand if she thinks I'm not listening. Miss Blandeau always did that with the younger girls, but I hadn't felt it in years. I'm afraid what else she might do with that stick.

I saw Francine last night, her first visit since I've come to Winterbay. I'm so glad she found me. She appeared in my cell. She told me to be wary of Mother Angelica. I'm not sure why. She wouldn't say. She did say I mustn't ever tell Mother Angelica about seeing her.

Mother Angelica gave me another lecture about the Devil today. She says the whole world is under Satan's control, and she's the only one who can stop him. It's frightening. Is that why Francine warned me about her?

July 12

A young man was at Sunday dinner, not too much older than me. He has red hair and a sweet face. He smiled and winked at me. I was so nervous I couldn't look at him, but my heart started pounding. I don't know if any man has ever smiled at me like that, just rude whistles, like the janitor at St. Bridget's with his crooked leer and those bug eyes. I wish I could be rid of the memory of the janitor's face forever.

I asked Sister Joanne, and she said the man's name is Duncan. That's a nice name. He works at the lighthouse offshore. He's so lucky. All the birds fly around it during the day, and many nest out there on the rock. I would love to visit. What a wonderful place to fly from.

I looked up at Duncan, who stared intently at me as I read. His story, at least Pamela's angel sightings and Angelica's obsession with demons, was playing out. Their meeting and her impressions of him were there too. I was beginning to see Pamela in a different light. This shy girl whom Duncan talked about and who spoke to me through her diary didn't seem so scary, or resemble that malevolent, hate-filled face I'd seen on the beach. She'd lived a sad and lonely life, and I could only assume had been abused in some way by this "janitor" she spoke of. I didn't see how these two visions could be the same person.

Sept. 5

Mother Angelica said today that I can't become a real nun until I recognize my sins and rid myself of demons. I asked her how I could do that, and she said she would show me. She led me upstairs to a room beneath the bell tower and pulled down a ladder. We climbed up, and she opened a padlocked door. There's a tiny room, barely big enough to pace, with one round window. There's a bed, a rocking chair, and a cradle. Why is that here? Surely the pregnant girls don't come up. Mother Angelica said I must stay here and pray for forgiveness. Then she locked the door.

Sept. 6

I'm writing this now, back in my regular cell, but I'm more worried than ever that Mother Angelica will find my diary. I was so alone up in the tower. The room was very quiet, except for the loud ringing of the bell every hour. After six hours, Mother Angelica came to get me.

Sister Joanne visited today. She says I must endure. She's very nice. I want to be like her. I hope I've made the right choice. I am scared.

Sept. 8

It's been three days since I was up in the tower. I have done little but pray, eat, and sleep. I don't ever want to spend another minute in that terrible place, so I must prove to Mother Angelica that I am worthy. I can hear her coming; she clicks that pointer on the wall as she walks.

The dates in the diary tailed off, and I was no longer sure how much time passed between them.

Dear Diary,

It's Sunday, the best day of the week. After morning mass, which is better than daily because there are more people there, I walked on the beach and watched the seagulls swoop and soar over the water. They are so beautiful.

I think and hope that I may see Duncan again tonight at dinner. I've been watching the lighthouse for any sign he is there or coming over in the little boat I see tied up at a small pier.

Duncan is here. I saw him arrive. I wanted to rush down to greet him, but that's forbidden. I'm not allowed to even speak with him when the others are there, let alone by ourselves.

Dear Diary,

Francine seems to really like Duncan, and she encouraged me to speak to him. Duncan baked me something he calls a Welsh cake. It is so delicious! I got sugar on my nose but never noticed. Duncan was so sweet trying to tell me.

Mother Angelica keeps an eye on me all the time.

Another girl has arrived, with child, and Mother Angelica has spent more time with her. I hope Mother Angelica has not taken her to that horrible tower room, but I fear she has. She brings everyone there to make them pray, to rid them of their demons.

Perhaps I can risk talking to Duncan. If Francine thinks I should, then I will.

Dear Diary,

I did it! I spoke with Duncan! He's so sweet and kind, and shy. We had trouble saying anything because we were both blushing so much. Sadly, we didn't have much time before Mother Angelica came nosing around. I don't think she saw.

I manage to talk to Duncan most Sundays now, briefly. Those conversations are the joy of my days, that and of course when I can talk to Francine. Duncan's from Wales, and has the loveliest accent. He's only lived here for a short while and is still unused to America. I find myself dreaming at night of showing him everything I know about the U.S., little as it is.

I told Duncan about my angels. I've never done that before. I've always been afraid of being called a liar, or worse, but he smiled and said I've been given a great gift. I'm so happy he understands! Maybe they will visit him too!

Pamela's diary took a turn at that point. Duncan must have guessed how far in I was. He swallowed another drink.

I don't know what I'm going to do. Last night, I was speaking with Francine, and Mother Angelica overheard me. She pulled me out of bed, and I spent the night and the next day in the tower, on my knees, praying. Mother Angelica says Francine's not an angel, but a demon in disguise. It's tricking me, playing on my foolishness. My soul is lost if I cannot send it away. She beat my bare feet with a rod to help me concentrate on my sins. What am I going to do?

Mother Angelica is more and more insistent that I am cursed, and plagued by demons, and my soul is in peril. She says the "voices" I hear, my angels, will lead me to terrible sin. But they are my only friends, besides Duncan. When will I see him again? I don't know what to do. I spend my days praying for guidance. The only direction I receive is either from Francine or Mother Angelica. Which way do I go? To whom do I listen? My soul depends on the truth. Please, God, let me see the truth. Perhaps Mother Angelica is right. I will not listen to my angels any longer. They are leading me astray.

Joanne gave me a letter today. It is from Duncan. He has asked me to go away with him. I am in despair. I love him so much, but I am going to be a nun. I have to. My angels are not here to help me know what to do.

I missed seeing Duncan today. I caught a glimpse of him from the tower window, but I must stay here until Mother Angelica lets me out.

Mother Angelica has let me out for the day. I feel as though I am near freeing myself of my demons, but I still keep this diary hidden. I will hide it under my clothes if I have to go back to that cell. I don't feel safe leaving it behind. Francine has not visited. Isn't that a sign that she is a demon?

I am sneaking out to see Duncan. He must know how I feel, but I still must tell him of my decision. How do I tell him?

I glanced up at Duncan again, wondering how often he reread this diary. How many years had gone by, and he still could not let it go?

There appeared to be a gap in the record at that point. Pamela made no mention of her visit to Duncan, but the aftermath was clear.

> *The tower has become my home. My belly grows bigger every day, with my "demon" as Mother Angelica calls it. I know now how wrong I was to trust her. I spend each lonely day hoping my angels will return to help me.*

> *Sister Joanne snuck some knitting needles and yarn to me. I am making a blanket, blue, with a tiny pretty heart on it for my baby. Mother Angelica says my baby will be given to a family to raise, and I will never see it. This made me cry. Please, Francine, help me. Don't let that evil woman have my baby.*

I stopped abruptly at that point. "That blanket?" I asked Duncan. "I found one just like it in the abbey. Is it Pamela's?"

Duncan's eyes went wide, and he dropped his cup. "You... you found a blanket?"

I nodded. "My first day here. It was in the room beneath the tower. Is it hers? It had a heart on it just like she describes here."

"No, no, it couldn't be," Duncan said, disbelief filling his voice. "I've been through every inch of that abbey. I would have seen it."

"Maybe not if Pamela's ghost left it there recently," I said.

"Keep reading," Duncan said in a low voice. "You'll see it isn't her."

I looked back at the diary, eagerly hoping for more answers and clues about the blanket. There was little left.

I could imagine Pamela, alone, afraid, her due date rapidly approaching, trying to write in her hidden diary in a dark tower room. She wavered back and forth, sometimes convinced she was possessed, resisting the idea at other times.

> *It's been six weeks. I'm so cold and hungry all the time. At least I'm no longer vomiting so much. I try to pray, but sometimes I just fall asleep. I know that's bad. I lie about it when Mother Angelica comes to see me. That's even worse. I must try harder to be rid of my demons. I know now that they caused me to be here, to be in my condition. I must fight them, control myself, or I will burn in Hell for sure. Mother Angelica is right. I am a bad person. I pray that Duncan will recognize his demons as well.*

> *I've made a mobile of pretty birds and hung it over the baby's cradle. Soon he, at least that's what I think he is, will love them as much as I do. I spend most of my time looking out the window, imagining I'm a bird, flying out to the lighthouse to see Duncan. Free.*

My angel returned today! Francine told me that Mother Angelica wants my baby, to hurt him, because she thinks he is the demon controlling me. She will kill him if she can. I don't know how, but I MUST SAVE MY BABY!

I asked the angel to take my baby, to keep him from Mother Angelica. She said she would. I am happy my baby will be safe.

Mother Angelica found the blanket I made. I am so frightened. Francine has told me that Mother Angelica has killed mothers here before and that I am next. I don't want to die.

Norman is back. He stands in the dark corner watching me sleep, watching the cradle. I'm so afraid. Afraid of the blood on my clothes. It's there. I saw it. He's still there.

It's so light up here, floating on the breeze, soaring over the sea. I'm free, free! My baby will never leave me. As soon as he learns to fly, we will both escape from here.

That was the final entry. Pamela had given up her baby, or had it taken, and died shortly thereafter, but there was no indication of that here, nor when she'd finally slipped from her own sanity. Her angels seemed like clear delusions, perhaps made up to help her get through her difficult times in the orphanage. The story was more than tragic, but I still wasn't completely convinced that Angelica was the ghost.

"Even if I accepted what you're saying about Angelica haunting the abbey," I said, "you still haven't answered my question. *Why* am I in danger?"

Duncan held his hand over his eyes. "There is no why, but it's always the same. Anyone who sees Angelica's ghost ends up dead. Mothers at the abbey, and girls ever since then, always around Halloween. Those she reveals herself to, die."

I remembered the Halloween tragedies—car driving into the bay, high school girl falling over a cliff into the surf on a dark night.

"They all saw her, during those Halloween bonfires."

"How do you know?" I asked.

"I know. Leave here and go home. You've seen her."

I ground my teeth. Duncan's theory sounded more like a way for him to clear his conscience. He'd failed Pamela and wanted to blame that failure on someone else. I stood up. "Thank you for the meal."

"You have to listen," he said, tears now streaming from his eyes. "I'm trying to help you."

I glanced at Duncan's tear-stained cheeks and the empty cup next to his hand. "If anyone needs help, it's you."

CHAPTER NINETEEN

I strode away from Duncan's cabin toward the path he'd led me on, enshrouded in damp darkness. The flashlight beam hardly helped as it reflected off the fog. I pulled out my phone to call Emily and tell her I might be late, if I could find my way back in the dark. No signal. Great. Lost in the woods and no service.

I put the phone in my jacket, still stewing over Duncan's lengthy story. He'd wasted my time without giving me any real answers.

But what if he was right?

Despite my dismissal of his warning, I had doubts about the ghost.

Who had I really seen on the beach? I was pretty sure it was Pamela. I tried to think back to all those ghost shows Emily watched. Could spirits manifest as different people? Maybe Angelica had somehow posed as Pamela.

But why would she do that? It didn't make a whole lot of sense. I couldn't believe I was even entertaining these thoughts.

Duncan did believe that Angelica remained after death to kill as she'd done in life. The abbey was her hunting ground.

Angelica was always looking for her next victim so she could drive the demons from their souls. All that seemed clear from the diary and her tombstone.

Though the more I thought about all this, the more his tale of a serial killer nun seemed like nonsense. The abbey was a tragic spot, and Pamela's diary certainly indicated Angelica had a disturbed personality. But could Pamela's account even be trusted? Her "angels" didn't indicate the most stable mind.

I'd stumbled into a nest of madness.

If the ghost was Angelica, she wouldn't have any reason to come after me. I didn't have any demons that needed driving out, nor did I claim to see angels like Pamela.

Maybe the only reason I'd seen a ghost was because I had spent so much time at the abbey. It had to be a coincidence. Although, Duncan lived next door and had explored every inch of the convent; he'd never seen a ghost.

Maybe I was just lucky.

Or unlucky.

Still, as I walked through the dark woods, Duncan's words rang through my head: *Anyone who sees her ends up dead.*

The breeze picked up.

I scanned the forest. A wide panorama of cobweb-like mist and trees populated the scene. A noise broke my thoughts. I squinted as rain pelted my face. The sound was a thud—like someone had thrown a large stone on the dirt. I thought I saw movement next to a bush, but the shadows crept into the spaces everywhere, making me doubt what I was seeing.

I quickened my pace, hurrying through the woods away from the noise. After running along the path for about two minutes, the trail forked. Confusion gnawed at me. *Which one leads back to the beach?*

A flock of birds erupted from the undergrowth, flapping toward the sky. I waited for them to pass, then glanced around looking for the main path that Duncan had lead me along. The landscape looked so different coming from this direction, especially in darkness and mist. I took the trail toward the left, hoping it would lead to the beach. After a minute of rushing, I heard the sound of waves crashing through the woods. Winding my way back through the thick-standing trees, I managed to reach the shore. I ran faster. Carefully trekking over the pebbled beach, I saw the abbey come into view on the dark cliffside. I shivered at the sight of the building. That place could fall off the outcrop into the ocean for all I cared.

I ran up the beach. I was now completely soaked from the rain and wishing I was in my car with the heater blasting. Out of breath, I made my way up a small hill away from the shore and found myself once again in that small copse by the cemetery. A thick mist hung low over the headstones. My lungs burned as I leaned on a tree to catch my breath. As I breathed deeply, the cold gripped me, and I sensed a presence. I looked back to see if Duncan had followed me. No one was in sight.

Another noise echoed from the depths of the forest: a loud, high-pitched vibration, like the tuning-fork sound I'd heard in the tower room. The pulsing noise magnified and I tried to steady myself. I wanted to run away, but the forest grew silent except for an odd scraping sound. My whole body went rigid when a movement beneath the trees caught my eye.

Some thirty feet away, a black silhouette stood hunched over Pamela's grave. My feet rooted to the ground as I stared, trying to make out who it was. The figure was small-framed and dressed in a nun's black habit. It made deliberate movements while the scraping sound intensified.

"Hello?" I managed to choke out.

The figure looked up. I couldn't make out the face. It tilted its head back and wailed a high-pitched scream, like the cry of a banshee. I covered my ears, wincing in pain, sure that my skull would crack at any moment. The sound pierced me, gripping my heart. I was surrounded by a deep malevolence that tore at my soul. I fell to my knees.

The shriek stopped.

I glanced up, and the figure was gone, enveloped by fog. The cemetery and surrounding woods were empty. A slight breeze wafted through the branches. I waited for perhaps five minutes, unsure if it was even safe to move. I should have run for the car, but just like in the tower room, my curiosity got the better of me. Mustering up all my courage, I walked toward Pamela's grave.

I shined my light at the marker. Carved in the stone was a new epitaph: *I have fought the good fight.*

CHAPTER TWENTY

As I sped along the winding road back to town, my tires slipped and spun on the wet road.

I tried to keep terror from overtaking me while hoping to make sense of what had just happened. The scene at the cemetery kept replaying in my mind.

What did it all mean?

Whoever the ghost was, she was dressed like a nun and had hovered over Pamela's grave. But unlike the time on the beach, I saw no face. Though that same sense of malevolence had filled the air, hatred so vile it hurt to think about.

The epitaph on Angelica's grave was now written on Pamela's: *I have fought the good fight.*

The ghost had obviously etched it onto Pamela's stone.

It could only have been Angelica.

Duncan was right. Angelica hated Pamela, even in death. Perhaps she carved her own epitaph on Pamela's grave as some declaration of triumph or justification for her actions. Or could the carving mean something completely different, something I didn't understand? Despite Duncan's story, the diary, and now this, I still was floundering to make heads or tails of the situation.

I wiped cold sweat from my forehead and stepped on the gas that much harder. All the way back to the hotel, I kept glancing in my rearview mirror, terrified that Angelica might somehow appear in my back seat or come flying after the car.

I wasn't sure how, but I made it back to the hotel without incident.

Sitting in the parking lot to collect myself, I arranged for plane tickets home on my phone to quell the sheer fear racing through my body. I'd finish the project for Ted and James, but there was no way in hell they were going to see me again unless it was in Seattle. There had been too many deaths and frightening incidents. Emily and I had to get away from here.

I ran upstairs and bounded into our room. Emily sat facing away from me on the chair next to the bed, her overstuffed knitting bag on the floor. She didn't even say hello. Instead, she stared at her twisted right hand as it lay draped across her belly. Then she held it up and slowly flexed her fingers.

"Emily?" I asked.

I wasn't sure what to say to her, except that this was our last night in Winterbay. Hopefully she wouldn't be too upset about our sudden departure. I didn't need another blowup.

I stood behind her, wondering when she'd notice me. She continued to stare at her hand, unmoving, unblinking.

"Em?" I said more loudly, walking in front of her. "Hey, something's come up, and we're heading home tomorrow. Let's get everything ready to go." I braced myself, waiting for her reaction.

She didn't look up. "Did you learn anything more about Pamela?"

I took off my coat and tossed it on the bed, amazed and grateful she hadn't launched into questions of why we were leaving or telling me we needed money. "Plenty. Too much, in fact. The abbey is a far more terrible place than I'd imagined. Forced adoptions, suspicious deaths, evil nuns, you name it. I can tell you all about it, but we need to start packing."

She set her knitting needles aside. "We're leaving? What about Pamela?" she asked again. "What does she need from us?"

I leaned over. Putting my hand under her chin, I gently turned her head toward me. Her eyes seemed a little blank.

"That's just the thing," I said. "I don't think the ghost is Pamela at all, or at least I'm not sure."

She blinked and shook her head. "Of course it's Pamela. You saw her. How could it not be?"

I let go of her chin. "I talked to Duncan, the man I told you about who I saw on the beach. He was…he knew Pamela, found her when she died."

Emily continued to stare. "Duncan," she whispered. Then she nodded. "In the water."

"Yes," I said. "Duncan thinks she was killed by the Mother Superior at the abbey, Angelica. The one whose death notice we saw in the newspaper. I'm sure you remember."

Emily nodded again, her eyes growing dark.

"Duncan thinks this Angelica is the ghost. He says she was responsible for Pamela's death. Pamela was pregnant, too. Duncan was the father. Angelica killed her, along with who knows how many other pregnant girls at the abbey. According to Duncan, Angelica has carried on her legacy, killing even after her death. I guess she was obsessed with demons and killed Pamela because she thought her baby was one."

I waited to see Emily's reaction, but she had none.

"Did you hear what I said?" I asked. "Pamela had a child."

Emily nodded. "That has to be the answer. Pamela wants us to find her baby."

"*What*? Why would you think that? And I told you—I don't think it's Pamela's ghost I've been seeing."

Emily shrugged. "It has to be. It's the only thing that makes sense. She wants her baby. That's what *I* would want."

My brain mulled over Emily's idea. Pamela wanting me to help her find her baby had never occurred to me. I might have accepted this idea yesterday, but in light of Duncan's story and what I'd seen at the cemetery, I wasn't sure any longer. I shook my head. "Even if you're right, we can't help her. We're leaving. Duncan warned me that everyone who's seen that ghost has ended up dead. Girls at the abbey, teens at those Halloween parties. We're not taking the chance." I stood up and reached for my suitcase.

Emily sighed, her eyes focusing. She rose from the chair and put her arms around my shoulders. "Okay, I understand. This whole experience has been frightening. It's time to go. I trust you," she whispered in my ear. She kissed me on the neck and squeezed me.

I touched her cheek and looked into her eyes, stunned by her compassion.

"Will, sorry I've been acting so strange. I haven't been feeling myself since I got here. I just want to get home."

I squeezed her, wishing more than anything we were on the damn airplane instead of in this stupid hotel. "Thank you. I almost can't function without your support right now," I said. I hugged her closer. "I love you more than anything."

"I know, and I love you too," she said.

I took her hands and smiled.

In that moment, I knew deep-down that we were going to be okay.

After a few more hugs, we did some packing and then grabbed a quick bite at the diner down the street. Before we went out, I called Ted and James. They wanted to meet for dinner tonight. I lied, saying Emily wasn't feeling well and I'd have to meet them another time, but that I'd finished all my scans and would get the plans to them.

At the restaurant, I filled Emily in with more of the details of finding the adoption records and meeting Duncan. She seemed overwhelmed by the sadness of it all, but whenever I mentioned Angelica, her face grew cold and distant. I felt much the same way about the old nun.

"So, do you believe Duncan?" she asked. "How could Angelica fool you? On the beach, I mean. You were so certain it was Pamela."

I nodded. "I know. Maybe I was mistaken. It's possible. Maybe the nun's habit fooled me. And who knows what ghosts can do? There's no rulebook for them. Have you heard of them posing as other people on any of your TV shows?"

"I maybe heard of it once. Maybe….I don't know if it's that common, though. It does seem like people are often confused by certain spirits, and it takes a lot of guesswork to figure out who a ghost represents."

"Well, the ghost's identity aside, the more I learned about Pamela from Duncan and her diary, the more I saw her as a lost, lonely girl, frightened and abused by a madwoman. It's sad. She seemed so sweet. The malevolence I saw on that face at the beach, the hatred I felt from her glance…it couldn't have come from Pamela. Angelica was the one filled with hatred."

"Yes," Emily said under her breath. "Pamela was a beautiful soul. Angelica hated babies."

I shrugged. "Maybe. Pretty frightening if she did." I glanced at Emily's swollen belly. "All the more reason to leave as soon as we can."

"What about Pamela's baby? What happened to him?"

"He's long gone," I said. "Adopted. Duncan didn't have any idea where he went, or at least he didn't mention it."

"Let's find him," Emily said, a note of pleading in her voice. "One last thing, for Pamela." Then in a whisper, "Give her son his blanket. We still have it."

I stopped and stared for a moment, not sure what I'd heard. "We're leaving," I said, my early fear of Emily's reaction returning to punch me in the gut.

She smiled. "That doesn't matter. Let's do it for her memory, and for Duncan."

"But we're flying out tomorrow," I said again.

"We don't have to do it here, silly," Emily said with a smile. "You've heard of the internet? Every time I watch those ghost shows, they talk about the importance of honoring those people connected to the ghost…anyone who may have been harmed by the spirit. It helps…helps things settle, so to speak. We can look for him online."

I let out a deep breath. Adoption records were hard to find. *I was sure nothing would come from a search, but if Emily wanted to sleuth it up from the safety of our home, I guess that would be okay.* I played with my fork. "I have some adoption papers in the car. There may be more information there."

Emily reached across the table and touched my hand. "Thanks," she said. "This should help us and bring closure."

I leaned back. I really should have known Emily was always motivated by an honest desire to help. She was stressed and out of sorts for any number of reasons on this trip, but her good heart always showed through.

After dinner, we returned to the hotel and finished packing. I composed an email to Ted and James explaining that Emily was a little worse, that she wanted to see her own doctor, and be home for Thanksgiving. In the closing paragraph, I mentioned my scans had given me all I needed, I would work from home, and return in a couple of weeks. That was another lie, but I'd deal with that later. I hit "Send." Hopefully, my leaving would go over okay, and I'd still have a job when I got back to Seattle. If not, I would do everything within my power to find another one, even if it meant flipping burgers for a while.

At least by tomorrow evening Emily and I would be back home, and I'd never have to step foot in Winterbay Abbey again.

I slept more soundly than I had in months. When the alarm woke me, I rolled out of bed with as little movement as possible. I wanted to let Emily sleep. She would be uncomfortable on the plane and might not get much rest while we were in the air.

The wind outside had picked up since last night and rattled the window. I'd checked the forecast before we'd gone to bed, and the weather service had predicted another storm. Hopefully it wouldn't affect our travel plans.

I tiptoed toward the bathroom, turning to take a look at Emily's sweet face while she slept.

I blinked. The bed was empty. I glanced around the room. She was nowhere in sight. "Emily?" I called as I headed for the bathroom. The door was wide open. I clicked on the light. No one.

Weird. Maybe she was at the front desk getting a towel or something. I took a shower and got ready. She still hadn't returned. I headed downstairs.

"Can I help you?" the woman behind the front desk asked, still sleepy-eyed.

"You haven't by chance seen my wife, have you? Blonde, pregnant?"

She took a sip of her coffee and shook her head. "Nope."

I ran outside to the parking lot. The rental car was gone.

A sharp pain twinged at the base of my head as I ran back up to the room. I grabbed my phone to see if there was a text from Emily. Hopefully she'd maybe just run out to the store for something.

Nothing. No texts, or voicemails. I called her phone. A loud vibration buzzed near my feet. I glanced at Emily's side of the bed. A blue light illuminated the carpet. I reached down to get her phone when my eyes locked on her knitting bag next to it. It had fallen over, the contents spilled out. I sorted through the pile, and my palms began to sweat. One, two, three, four…. Blue baby blankets, complete with pink hearts, the fourth one half-finished and still connected to Emily's knitting needles. They were exact copies of the blanket I'd found at the abbey.

CHAPTER TWENTY-ONE

I tried not to panic as I stared out the windshield. Tiny flakes of snow swirled by the glass, whipped into a frenzy by a wind that seemed to be blowing at near-hurricane force. Ice crept up from the bottom corners to glaze half the window. I'd been so hurried to get in the car that I hadn't scraped the frost.

Thankfully, the woman at the front desk let me borrow her car. My made-up story about Emily going to the store and not returning must have stirred some compassion.

I sped down the road. My anxiety only increased in tune with the storm I was now barreling through. I tried to focus on Emily. I was positive she had gone to the abbey, but didn't know why. And the blankets…. What did all of this mean? Why had Emily knitted them? I thought back to all the times Emily had been knitting during this trip. As I thought about it, she'd had her hand in her knitting bag at every spare moment. It almost seemed like she'd been out of it, trance-like, whenever she was near that bag. A memory of Emily looking at Pamela's blanket for the first time popped into my mind. Emily really hadn't been the same since then. Was the blanket somehow a conduit, a link between the ghost and the people she haunted?

The blanket belonged to Pamela, but had Angelica been using it as a lure?

I'd also touched it. That could explain why I'd seen Angelica's ghost and Duncan hadn't.

I shook my head as I drove on. I didn't have all the answers. I needed to find Emily.

The road was icy, and I had to drive slower than I wanted. I'd risked death racing this road just last night. That lent me no assurance. I was still afraid I'd run the car off the road.

More snowflakes whisked across the pavement. With each gust the car bucked sideways, and a time or two I felt the tires slip and spin on the compact snow building up on the asphalt. I gripped the wheel until my fingers ached, trying to hold the car steady through the curves and cutbacks.

I sat up straighter when I pulled around a forested bend and spotted red and blue lights flashing ahead. A police car was parked behind a roadblock spanning the width of the road.

My heart jumped to my throat. The lights flashed just as they had that wet night when Emily and I had skidded into the telephone pole.

I pulled up to the roadblock, frightened to even look. There was no sign of any crash, just the patrol car. A rotund officer stood in front of the obstruction talking into his radio. He put it down when I pulled up.

I rolled down the window as he approached the car. His nose was bright red from the cold. "Mornin'," he said.

"What's happened here?" I asked. "Was there an accident?" I held my breath, imagining the wreck of a car just out of sight down the road.

"No. No accident. Where are you headed?" he asked gruffly.

I closed my eyes and thanked God. "The abbey," I said. "I work out there. I wondered if you happened to see a blonde woman driving a silver Subaru come through here?"

"No, no one has come through, at least not since the blockade has been up, about an hour ago. Why?"

"My wife…I think she may have—" I stopped short, wondering what to say. "I think she may have driven out to the abbey to look for me."

"Well, I can't let you pass. Not yet anyway. There's been a robbery at the quarry," the officer said.

"*Robbery*? Someone stealing rocks?" Seemed strange that the police would be throwing up roadblocks for pilfered stone.

The cop took a step back. "It'll be a couple of hours till we have this cleared," he said, ignoring my question.

"I can't wait. We have a plane to catch."

He glanced down the road toward the abbey. "Sorry. I can't let you through."

I slapped the wheel, my fingers red with cold and now frustration. "I have to get through!"

He put his hand on his sidearm. "I'll have to ask you to exit the vehicle." Then he mumbled into his radio. I froze as another cop approached and looked into the window.

"You again?" Vaughn asked, annoyed. "What's the problem?"

"Please, I have to get to the abbey. I think my wife may have driven out there to look for me and gotten lost. She's pregnant. I'm worried about her."

At the word "pregnant" Vaughn stiffened. "You never mentioned she was pregnant."

"Is that important?"

"Look, the abbey, that place…" He paused, gritting his teeth and leaning into the window. "All those teen rituals, the accidents I told you about…we never knew, but…" He stopped again and looked away. "All those girls, they claimed to see a nun, like you did. The ones who died, they were all pregnant, and oddly they all had…"

He trailed off without finishing his thought.

"What?" I asked, now extremely fearful.

"Never mind. It's inconsequential."

My heart stopped. "They all had knitted baby blankets, didn't they? The same one?"

"Yeah, how did you know?" he asked.

I opened Emily's purse and held up a blanket.

Vaughn's face drained of blood.

I threw the car into gear.

He yanked the barrier out of my way.

"I can't leave just yet, but I'll follow as soon as I can!" he called after me.

I raced off, my chest pounding as Vaughn's words sunk in. Why hadn't I figured this out earlier and left days ago? I'd given the blanket to Emily. This was my fault.

Why hadn't Vaughn seen Emily? This was the only road. How long had she been out at the abbey? It had been longer than an hour at least. Horrific ideas of what might have happened to her swept through my mind. I pressed my foot down on the accelerator. *Please be okay.*

I finally made it to the turn to the abbey and hurried up the long drive. The wind was even more violent here near the shore than back in town. I had to hold the steering wheel hard as the car was rocked by the fierce weather. Tree limbs whipped in a frenzy all around the property.

As I drove toward the parking lot, I scanned the grounds. There was no one in sight, and nothing looked out of the ordinary. No rental car either.

When I jumped out of the car, the sharp crosswind cut through me, chilling my core. Hard-driven snow stung my face like a thousand tiny bee stings. I winced. The temperature was even colder than the water the day I witnessed the drowning.

I made it to the front entrance then stopped quickly. A silver Subaru was parked on the grass around the back of the abbey. I sprinted toward it. Snow dusted the windows. "Emily!" I called as I opened the driver's side. No one was there.

I glanced around. No sign of anyone anywhere.

She had to be inside the abbey.

I grabbed my flashlight off the front seat of the rental and rushed toward the entrance. The door hung ajar. I hurried inside, terrified of what I might find.

CHAPTER TWENTY-TWO

The abbey brooded, dark as a tomb. I ran up and down the first floor, shouting for Emily. No answer. I remembered her empty stares, her trance-filled blank eyes. If she was under Angelica's influence, she probably couldn't reply. I'd have to check every room in this damn cursed building.

I climbed down into the basement, shouting and shining the light on every inch of that terrible hole. Still no sign of Emily.

I made my way back upstairs as fast as I could and stopped near the front entrance. Small piles of wind-blown snow littered the floor beneath broken windows. The bright white color in the dark gave the hall a ghostly glow as it reflected my flashlight beam. Echoing down the hall and stairwell, a whiney, wind-born howl filled the corridors.

I started up the staircase, heading straight toward the tower room.

I reached the dorm room under the tower. The ladder descended to the floor, and a thin wire ran upward.

Something scraped above my head. My guts clenched. I imagined Angelica lurking up there, waiting for me.

I jumped as the wire tapped against the ladder.

"Emily?" I called, shining my light into the darkness above. "Emily? Are you there?"

A grunt and short string of curse words in a Welsh accent followed my questions.

"Duncan!" I called.

When I reached that dingy little prison cell where Pamela had been tortured and abused, I jumped back. Duncan stood over me. He held a spool of wire in his hands. The space was dimly lit and otherwise looked exactly as I'd left it—bed, cradle, and paper mobile of birds.

"What are you doing here? Where's my wife?!" I shouted.

Duncan, confronted by my sudden appearance and flash of anger, shuffled backward. "What do you mean, where is your wife?" he asked.

"My wife," I said again. "Young, blonde, pregnant. Her car is right outside. She's in here. What have you done with her?"

Duncan eyed me for a long moment. His expression looked even wearier than when I last saw him. "I didn't even know you had a wife."

"She came looking for me. Where is she?!"

"I haven't seen her, but if she's pregnant I can damn well say who has," he mumbled, his voice thick and hoarse like he hadn't slept in days. His whole body shook, and I could smell alcohol on his breath. "I *knew* something would happen," he said. "But you didn't listen."

"I'm listening now. Where would Angelica take her?"

He turned his head toward the window.

At this slight movement, he didn't have to tell me. I knew.

I ran to the window, open now because I'd knocked out the bricks two days before. A narrow view of the beach was all I could see. The small part of the shoreline in my line of sight was empty, but that didn't mean Emily wasn't down there.

"Get out, now!" Duncan shouted. "I'm going to end all this." He dropped the wire onto the floor. I glanced along its length. The end ran under the bed frame. A bundle of what looked like dynamite lay beneath. He pushed past me, slid down the ladder, and thumped onto the floor below.

I thought back to Vaughn up the road. Had explosives been what was missing from the quarry? Maybe Duncan had stolen them, and wired the tower—and probably the entire building—to explode. I didn't see any detonator on him, but I figured the abbey was soon to be a pile of rubble.

I jumped down the hatchway and raced past him.

"The drownings, the deaths. She can't be allowed to harm anyone else," he called after me.

I had no objections. I only wished he'd done it years ago.

CHAPTER TWENTY-THREE

In a blind panic, I ran out of the abbey. I turned toward the beach and sprinted to the slope leading down to the water. The wind had picked up, biting and salt-scented, still flinging shard-like flakes of snow at me. I tried to cover my face from the burning sensation.

Everything was clear now: Angelica had used me to lure Emily here, where her powers were probably at their strongest. The blanket was some kind of supernatural snare. I'd let it entrap me, then given it to Emily. Perhaps my having a pregnant wife had been a terrible coincidence, or maybe Angelica could tell somehow, read my mind or something. Why hadn't I seen? Why?

I ran on.

Reaching the path on the cliff, I looked toward the beach.

The silhouette of a woman dressed in black contrasted sharply against the fog and white shoreline. In front of her, another woman wearing a long white nightgown was inching away. The woman's damp nightshirt clung to her body, accentuating her belly.

"Emily!" I yelled. My voice was lost on the wind. *She will freeze out here.*

I kept running down the path but had to slow over patches of ice forming on the already slick rocks.

Finally I reached the bottom. A jolt hit me from behind, and a sharp pain began to throb at the base of my skull. "Oww!" I put my hand to my neck. Something oozed wet and warm against my frozen hand. I glanced at my palm. Blood.

A loud shriek sounded over my head. I looked up through the snow. Dozens of seagulls flew against the wind with a fierceness that overmatched the wild weather. They circled, riding the frozen air currents, wings outstretched, hovering above me. Eyes black yet somehow alight, their jagged razor beaks opened and called out.

One of them dove straight for me.

I threw my arms in front of my face and jumped out of its way.

The maniacal thing hit the rocks with a muffled crack, breaking its neck.

The birds had to be crazed, just like the one in the hotel parking lot and the flock that had mysteriously come out of nowhere inside the abbey.

I looked down the beach.

Emily edged closer to the water. The waves crashed against the shore, wild as the birds, and washed around her feet.

The ghost turned toward me. I saw the face of the girl from the newspaper article. Angelica—posing as Pamela—waved toward the seagulls and then at Emily.

I ran to Emily.

A shriek rang out and another sharp pain tore at the top of my head.

"Dammit!" I yelled as the seagull swooped away, my blood staining its beak.

Another dove. I lashed out, and it struck my arm, a hammer blow. It flew away, and yet another hurled itself at me. I blocked this strike as well, but the bird's beak ripped into my forearm. I could barely take a step under the assault.

They would kill me if Angelica kept up this attack.

"Emily!" I shouted again.

Her ankles were now in the water, and I could see that she held something blue in her hand. Pamela's blanket.

My blood ran cold. I swatted away another bird and took off again.

There was another lacerating peck. This time at the top of my ear. I cried out and held my head.

Again. This one on my forehead.

Emily was now knee-deep in the water.

Angelica kept waving.

Emily edged further away, but not before she looked back at me. There was a flash of recognition in her eyes.

"Emily, please, fight back! She's trying to kill you!" I screamed.

Just then something struck me, but not from above. A burning, a sense of rage, but not my own, scorched my chest.

Get away from her, the voice of a woman called into my head.

I looked at Emily, and her expression blurred, pixelating into an old black and white photograph. There was no trace of her blonde hair and soft features. Instead, a young girl wearing a nun's habit, her look serious and unsmiling, stared at me from the water.

I stumbled backwards, trying to dodge another bird.

Emily opened her mouth. "You just missed your mom. She dropped off some of your childhood keepsakes!" she yelled.

The sound of a baby's rattle reverberated around me. The noise intensified. It morphed into the shrill tuning-fork sound, becoming deafening.

I covered my ears. "Stop!" I yelled. "Leave me alone! Leave Emily alone!"

"Stop!" Emily yelled, imitating my plea. "Leave me alone." The sound of intense rain hitting pavement replaced her voice. She pointed at me. "Will, watch out! The motorcycle. It's going to hit us! Stop! Stop!" Emily screamed.

All at once, the sound of glass shattering shrieked up and down the beach. I dropped to the rocky beach again as another bird pecked my arm. I screamed, and my eyes widened as a pool of blood formed on the ground.

Emily's monochrome face began to change and contort. Glimmers of normal, human flesh tones shone through.

She was fighting, but I didn't know how to help her, or myself.

Just then, Angelica stepped toward me, and I thought I would stop breathing. I stared at her face. "*Not you, nor anyone, is going to hurt her any more. She's going to fly away on angel's wings, out there,*" she said, pointing to the horizon. "*Norman won't have her again, or Mother Angelica. No one will be able to take her baby away.*"

Pamela?

Duncan had been wrong.

This ghost was not Angelica.

Emily was now waist deep.

Another bird dive-bombed me, this time on my thigh. I held my leg as blood seeped into my jeans.

I pointed toward the abbey. Now that I knew for sure who the ghost was, I screamed to be heard in the wind. "Duncan is up there. He wants to be with you. Go to him, and leave us alone! Emily doesn't need to be protected! Your tormentors are dead, gone. They can't hurt anyone."

Pamela didn't move.

Instead, my voice began to echo back toward me, slowed, distorted.

I glanced over at Emily. Her face was now back to normal, but her neck was bent awkwardly, and she was staring at me. Her mouth moved, and I heard my own voice come out. "Emily doesn't need to be protected!" she cried with my voice.

My fear and frustration became violent rage, spewing up in my throat. Before I knew what I was doing, I charged at Pamela.

As I got closer to her, a strong surge of current pulsed through my body. She tried to move away, but I drove headfirst into her, intent on knocking her down. A shock wave rippled through all my limbs. I closed my eyes. The world vanished as Pamela screamed.

I opened my eyes. The beach reappeared, transformed, the world emerged in black and white, a faded universe devoid of color and depth. There was no snow, no cold. Only a sea that looked like blue flame, a burning pit of fire. Where was I? Was this Pamela's reality?

When I stared at Emily out in the surf, all I could see was a white figure in the flames, shifting and undulating in pulses of light. A black fog enveloped her head and the hand holding the blanket. Ebony tendrils extended all the way from Emily toward Pamela's waving hands.

I ran toward Emily, but when I reached the black fog it pushed me back.

I looked back at Pamela. "You have to stop. Please."

Pamela glanced back at me. This time I didn't see a malevolent face. Instead, her face was pained, frightened. This was the eighteen-year-old girl who'd lost everything. The girl who had been locked away in a small room, shunned by people she trusted, tortured by those she'd feared.

I looked out toward the waves. Emily's figure edged further out into the bay. She would be under the waves any minute.

I stumbled toward Pamela and fell to my knees.

"Please, it's not too late. You don't have to protect any more girls. No one can ever hurt you again. If you've ever loved someone, please don't do this. You can still find peace. Let me save her. She's my wife. I love her."

"You don't deserve love," Pamela said through her tears. *"No one does."*

Her words cut through me, a burning sword of hatred, but somehow I forced myself to move. I staggered up and started running. Not toward Pamela or Emily, but to the black fog that connected them. If I broke the connection, maybe it would free Emily from Pamela's stranglehold.

As I stepped in front of the haze, I was again stopped cold. Voices pierced my thoughts as the fog enshrouded me. Women sang soft lullabies, children cooed. The blanketing warmth of a summer day flowed around me, followed by images of children swimming in pristine lakes and pools. I felt pulled, coaxed, and caressed in ways I hadn't felt since I was a child. *I could only guess Pamela was broadcasting these thoughts at Emily, luring her out to sea with a false sense of security.*

How could I break this chain? Was it possible in this weird netherworld to cast my own thread into Pamela's net?

I closed my eyes and thought of Emily. Images of the day we first met, our first night together, our wedding, the day the babies were conceived—all spun through my mind and out toward Emily.

"Hear me," I whispered. "I'm here."

My voice wavered, was overawed. As I spoke, Pamela's idyllic, hate-filled fantasy towered over mine.

"Drop the blanket!" I screamed at Emily.

Emily stared, unhearing.

I pushed my thoughts again to Emily, but she showed no recognition. The water was up to her chest. In my despair, I started thinking of Duncan and replayed everything he'd told me at his cabin to direct toward Pamela. All his anguish, laid bare for her to see.

When I conjured the image of Duncan drunk and crying for her, all the voices and thoughts diminished, ever so slightly.

"*No!*" came a distorted cry. Pamela moved, repositioned the tendrils binding her to Emily.

I moved in the way of the black fog one more time, again thinking of Duncan.

"*You're just like him!*" she screamed at me. "*You never wanted your baby. Neither did he. He left me to rot, just as you would have left her. Don't pretend to care.*"

"That's not true! Duncan loved you and the baby. He didn't know what Angelica was doing. He was respecting your wishes to be left alone. Like him, I want to be a father. Everyone has a moment of weakness, and I had mine, but it means nothing now."

"*And nothing is what you will have,*" she snarled. A wave of her hand threw me to the ground.

I faced the sea. The brightness of Emily's body almost blinded me. I crawled to my feet and stumbled toward her. "I love you!" I yelled. "And our babies! Don't let her have you. Please, forgive me."

Emily looked at me, and I could see her eyes shining with recognition. "I do," she said.

I closed my eyes for an instant and then turned to Pamela, determined to die to stop her. With all the strength I had left, I lunged at her.

A terrible shriek rang out.

All at once, I was everywhere and nowhere, falling into a vortex, dividing into an infinity of parts.

A loud crack burst in my ears.

I lay face down on the beach, water slapping my face. Snow fell, whipped by the wind at horrendous speed. The seagulls flew away, unable to withstand the tempest. Color returned. Blood red.

I lifted my head, and my mouth dropped at the sight in front of me.

On the cliff, an orange glow enveloped the abbey as an inferno blasted through the roof, raging into the sky.

CHAPTER TWENTY-FOUR

Smoke and flame roared from the abbey like an avenging angel. The old building cried in agony as fire blackened its skin, broke its bones. Another explosion racked the south end, and the bell tower collapsed in on its pyre.

He'd done it. Duncan had actually blown the damn place up.

I stood up immediately, turned away from the howling disaster, and searched for Emily in the foaming surf. I'd nearly freed her from Pamela's grasp when the blast struck.

Neither Emily nor Pamela was anywhere to be seen. Had the abbey's destruction broken Pamela's hold on this world?

"Emily!" I scrambled to my feet. "Emily!"

Wind-driven waves crashed on the beach at my feet. "Emily!" I scanned the surf. There was still no sign of her, Pamela, or any threatening seagulls.

Had she gone under? I plunged into the sea, not thinking of the numbing cold. Pain shot up through my legs until I lost all feeling. I continued to swim in the direction of where I'd last seen her.

Finally, I came up for air, and a wave cascaded onto me, forcing me down again. I swam to the surface and glanced out to the horizon.

No one was in sight.

Shouting until my voice grew hoarse, I stumbled out of the water and ran up and down the beach in search of my wife.

The sound of the howling wind was the only response to my calls.

I fell to my knees onto the rocks.

The police found me there, lying on the beach, waves washing over me. I don't recall much else. Later, a nurse told me that a giant Saint Bernard lay next to me, keeping me from freezing to death. Vaughn dragged me to the ambulance that rushed me to Winterbay hospital. I'd suffered from severe hypothermia, frostbite in my hands and face, and multiple lacerations.

I'd nearly died, the nurse added. I wished I had. There was no sign of Emily. So far, the only remains they'd discovered were Duncan's among the ruins of the abbey. The police said Duncan was clutching a gold necklace with a cross pendant charm, a slight smile on his face.

The next day, when I finally awoke, my hands were covered in bandages, and I lay propped up in bed. The nurse took my temperature and asked if I was warm enough as she checked the drip on my I.V. "Two men are here to see you, if you feel up to it," she said, a sweet smile on her face. "I'll send them away if you want to be alone." She took my gauze-covered hand in hers.

"Ted and James?" My voice sounded as though it came from someone else. I was too numb to say no.

The nurse nodded and opened the door for them. She looked back at me. "I'll be just outside if you need anything. The button is right there in your hand."

The two walked in together, holding hands. Ted stood over me and bit his quivering lip. "Will…I, I don't know what to say. I'm so sorry." He looked away.

James stepped up next to him and patted me on the arm. "It was that crazy beach guy, the lighthouse keeper."

"Duncan," I said.

"Yeah, Duncan," James went on. "He had some grudge or other, the police said. They also said he stole explosives from the quarry and wired the whole building. He must have set it off just as you arrived. You're lucky you weren't inside. Although…."

I swallowed, my throat raw and dry. "I know," I said. "I did go inside. I saw the wiring and Duncan."

Ted turned back around. "You did? Then you got out just in time. Do you know why he did it?"

I looked away. What could I tell them? It's not like I could explain that Duncan had destroyed the abbey to rid the world of a malevolent, vengeful spirit. "It's my fault," I cried, choking back tears.

"*Your* fault?" Ted said. "How could it be your fault? You may have caught him in the act, but there was no way to have known beforehand he'd go off half-cocked."

"I never should have brought Emily here," I said, shame overwhelming me.

Ted put his hand on my arm.

I wanted to crawl under the bed and hide. "Why didn't I see? The cradle, the knitted heart, those other girls…."

Ted and James glanced at each other. Quizzical looks spread over their faces.

"What do you mean?" James asked.

"Winterbay," I said, not even sure I was making sense. "Cursed," was all I could muster.

CHAPTER TWENTY-FIVE

Time almost stood still for me.

Ted and James drove me to the airport a week later. Gryffin sat next to me, his head resting on my lap. Ted and James had adopted him after they found him whimpering over his dead master.

I patted Gryffin while my thoughts turned back to Emily. She was all I could think of. I hadn't been able to rest. She was in every thought and dream. The nurses had taken care of me as best they could before I left for home. In some ways, I didn't want to leave the hospital. How was I even going to go on living after this?

Standing near the ticket counter at the airport, James stepped forward. "I really hate to bring this up now. It seems so cold, but with you now leaving….We just wanted you to know that we plan to completely rebuild the abbey, or rather the hotel. We're going to start from scratch. The property is too nice to let go."

I nodded and continued to shuffle through the line. "I'm sure it will be a huge success for you," I said, numbly.

"We still want to use your ideas, and we hope you'll see them through, you know, adapting to a completely new structure," Ted said.

I was surprised they were even telling me this right now. It did seem insensitive. I really couldn't think straight.

"We realize how painful this place may be for you. There's no need to come back. You can do everything from Seattle. And if you choose not to, we completely understand."

"Yes," James continued for him. "And…we have more projects we'd like you to consider if this one is too…too hard. Sorry, I'm sure that came out all wrong."

I held out my hand and shook both of theirs. "Thank you," I said. "I'll think about it." I turned away, determined never to see Winterbay again.

CHAPTER TWENTY-SIX

Three weeks had passed since Emily's death. Her body was never found. I had to admit that gave me some false hope, though the logical part of my brain knew she most likely drowned and washed away with the tide in that cursed bay.

Sometimes I'd wake up in the middle of the night reaching out for her, only to find her clothes I'd wadded up on her side of the bed. Putting words to the guilt, loss, and grief I felt was impossible. I'd had to teach myself how to do the simplest things, almost like relearning how to tie my shoes. I hadn't even taken off the sweater Emily made me since I'd returned to Seattle.

The worst part was the memorial. A lot of people came, so many artists; Emily was well-liked. Some brought drawings and paintings instead of flowers, more reminders of how creative she'd been. Ariel stopped by as well. She made soup for me and said she would help in any way she could. She finished by saying that it's what Emily would have wanted. I was grateful for Ariel's kindness, but didn't feel I deserved it.

After the memorial, Emily's mother Sharon came by. We both cried as we packed up things she wanted. I didn't really like Sharon taking anything. Having everything in the house just as it was somehow kept Emily alive for me.

Emily was all Sharon had left, though. Who was I to tell her she couldn't have some of her daughter's things?

After about half an hour of packing, Sharon excused herself and walked outside with a box of tissues. Shortly after, I heard her drive off without Emily's things.

I haven't seen her since. *I guess everyone has to deal with grief in their own way.*

Besides the incessant emotional tugging in all different directions, life was quiet. I went back to work, unable to stand any more silence.

My first day in the office, Lance called me in. This time by phone.

"Hey, Will, I need to see you for a moment," he said.

"Okay," I said. A nervous twinge began to churn my stomach.

I prayed this wasn't the last meeting Lance and I would have. *I could guess the demise of the abbey hadn't sat well with him.*

I walked into his office.

He gestured for me to sit down.

A concerned look came over his face. "How're you holding up?" he asked.

"I'm…I don't know how to answer that question. I'm alive. That's pretty much all I can say," I replied.

He sat back in his chair and nodded. A good twenty seconds passed before he spoke again. "I just got an email from Ted and James. I'm not trying to be pushy, and if you want to take more time off, please feel free, but they were asking if you wanted to continue work for them on their new hotel out in Winterbay."

I cleared my throat. I'd forgotten about their request.

"They're specifically asking for you, and if I didn't know any better, their email seemed to hint at wanting you for other projects as well."

I nodded.

"Look, I'm more than happy to give this to someone else if that's what you want," he said.

By "someone else," he meant Dustin. I wasn't about to let that prick just pick up my ideas and take all the credit for them again. Besides, Ted and James were adamant about not wanting to work with anyone but me.

I adjusted my collar. Perhaps, in some strange way, actively creating something new would help me heal. Emily would have wanted that. I was sure of it. I wouldn't go back to Winterbay; Ted and James had said I could work remotely from Seattle.

I glanced at Lance.

He was staring at me.

"I think I will go ahead with it," I said.

He smiled. "Okay. Good. And there's no problem with staying here to complete everything," he said.

"Thanks," I said.

I walked back to my desk past Noelle, who was on the phone. She gave me a sorrowful smile.

I brought out my original sketches of the hotel. The abbey was still the summer wonderland hotel from the 1890s I originally envisioned.

Readying myself for a long session of work, I took a very slow breath. It was going to be good to be productive again. I wanted to draw a new, different building that would take advantage of the site. I had no desire to keep anything from that dark past, but only use it as a reference.

I put my Winterbay drawings on the desk. After I took out my pens and a new sheet of paper, I peered at my old sketch.

A jolt pulsed through me as I studied the abbey's entryway.

A figure stood there, a woman. She cradled two small bundles in her arms.

I touched the soft image of Emily with my index finger and began to sob.

Through the tears, I glanced at the abbey's bell tower window.

Pamela was nowhere to be seen.

AUTHORS' NOTE

Henry James, Charles Dickens, H.P. Lovecraft, Washington Irving, Edgar Allan Poe, Joseph Sheridan Le Fanu, M.R. James. Just a few of the names you may recognize from the last two centuries as having populated imaginations with tales of Gothic horror, a genre we adore. There is nothing better than reading a Gothic supernatural story like "The Legend of Sleepy Hollow" or "The Fall of the House of Usher" by the faint light of a candelabrum. Classic tales like these defined Gothic horror and continue to inspire new stories, including recent films like *Crimson Peak*.

In addition to reading the classics, we are always on the lookout for modern writers who harken back to these old tales. English author Susan Hill's ghost stories (*The Woman in Black, The Small Hand, Dolly*) and John Boyne's novel, *This House is Haunted*, represent some of the best the genre has to offer today. Their tales follow the Gothic tradition in both time and place, although Gothic need not be relegated to Victorian or Edwardian England. The genre fits into the present as well, as long as a sense of forbidden, forgotten evil returning from the past, and a sense of place are retained.

John's love for horror and Gothic started early. His older brother told terrifying stories of haunted radio towers on the distant hill of his Spokane neighborhood. Hundred-foot-tall metal monsters with creepy red lights that glowed in the dark of night populated his nightmares. He also recalls sneaking peeks at the daytime Gothic soap opera *Dark Shadows* with its vampires, werewolves, and witches. The first book he ever read on his own was a collection of ghost stories.

In grade school, John put his love of horror to the test. He walked home every day past the local neighborhood haunted house where, his best friend's older brother told him, an insane teenager had murdered his family in their beds with a butcher knife. One day, along with his friend, John built up the courage to sneak inside the abandoned Lizzie Bordenesque-house. He pushed through the creaking door and made his way up the winding staircase as visions of the murdered family, and a madman wielding a knife danced in his head.

On the second floor, where the terrible deed had purportedly taken place, he peered into the bedrooms of the murdered. It was there that he confronted his greatest fear: an angry neighbor, tired of kids who believed in the made-up nonsense about a midnight murder. The neighbor chased John and his friend back into the street, leaving them to wonder if perhaps they had seen a ghost.

Not satisfied with the horror down the street, John developed a long love affair with the *CBS Radio Mystery Theater*, a radio anthology from the 1970s featuring scary audio tales and adaptations of classic ghost stories. The creaking door of the opening credits made up the soundtrack of his childhood, and undoubtedly left him susceptible to stories of haunted houses.

John introduced Davonna to radio drama some years back, and she's been entertained and frightened by spooky shows ever since. She grew up reading a healthy dose of Alvin Schwartz's *Scary Stories*, a staple at sleepover parties and Girl Scout meetings. She also read R.L. Stine's young-adult novels. Every year, Halloween rivaled Christmas in her holiday preparations. She hunted down Halloween decorations and festooned her home with spider webs and pumpkins in anticipation of All Hallow's Eve. Disney's classic 1949 cartoon, *The Legend of Sleepy Hollow* narrated by Bing Crosby, was a must-watch during the Halloween season along with Disney's animated *Halloween Treat* cartoons.

From the time she was five until the end of high school, Davonna owned a Disneyland pass and frequently went on the Haunted Mansion ride. She remembers being terrified—yet enthralled—with all the ghostly effects. Her freshman English teacher introduced her to Edgar Allan Poe, and she began to read his works, helping to solidify her love of all things classically Gothic and macabre.

This mutual love of creepy Gothic and ghost tales—coupled with our longstanding friendship—made it seem natural for us to co-write a ghost story. Two months before Halloween in 2014, we challenged each other to write a ghostly tale based on a list of supposedly haunted buildings and locations in the U.S. We settled on a combination of a haunted hotel and a lighthouse, which morphed into the Winterbay Abbey setting along with its brooding lighthouse offshore. Just like the fateful summer of 1816 at Lord Byron's Villa Diodati on Lake Geneva (the vacation mansion where Mary Shelley dreamed up her gothic masterpiece, *Frankenstein*, in response to a writing challenge), by the end of August we were on our way to creating our own Frankenstein story.

While *Winterbay Abbey* is a work of fiction, the idea surrounding it is partially rooted in history. We chose an abbey as the setting based on Davonna's research from her previous book, *Seeing Red*. Set in the 1960s, *Seeing Red* tells the story of a young woman navigating a pre-women's lib world. Davonna's investigation into that era led her to the discovery of a disturbing yet common practice for handling many unwed pregnant girls. Their ashamed families sent them to asylums or convents for the duration of their pregnancies to avoid public humiliation.

These asylums comprised an expansive institution throughout Europe and North America for much of the 19th and 20th centuries. They were an untalked-of secret that society knew were places for "bad girls." And they were often much more than places where middle-class daughters hid from shame. For the poor, they could become prisons with virtually no way out. Forced to purchase their freedom at often exorbitant prices, some girls were enslaved for many years.

Magdalene asylums or laundries, Irish institutions run by Catholic nuns that housed unwed mothers, prostitutes, and other "wayward girls," have become popularized by films like the *Magdalene Sisters* and *Philomena*. These movies dramatized life for the destitute and abandoned women living in convents. The films depict true horror, as women suffered incredible abuses and were robbed of their children and their freedom. A mass grave uncovered near one of the Magdalene laundries in Dublin, Ireland contained the bones of 155 forgotten women and children.

These facts stuck with Davonna. As she has a tendency to idealize the past, her *Sound of Music* image of happy singing nuns suffered a terrible blow.

Thus, we decided to make *Winterbay Abbey* a place of terror. While Winterbay itself has no mass graves, it still stands as a symbol of the struggles and abuses women faced at the hands of would-be reformers. Good Gothic stories usually allude to some familial or societal sin, and *Winterbay Abbey* is steeped in its own especially awful secrets. Furthermore, some early Gothic novels (*The Mysteries of Udolpho* by Ann Radcliffe and *The Monk* by Matthew Gregory Lewis) include nuns as mysterious central characters.

In addition to encompassing a dark lineage, good Gothic horror is also marked by often bleak, yet beautiful settings like the coast of Maine, making it the perfect place to host a ghostly tale. Gnarled trees like skeletal hands, fog that comes and goes on a whim, and the unforgiving sea are part of the region's personality. *Winterbay*'s setting truly became its own character.

And of course there is the abbey itself, a looming estate with a curse that eventually brings it down in a final disaster. Without a suitable building, dark and mysterious, decrepit and abandoned, Gothic horror is not as powerful, not even really Gothic. And while the coast of Maine provides a terrific setting, Winterbay Abbey itself sets the frightening scene as it looms above that wild, isolated shore.

As our setting, Winterbay Abbey had to evoke the proper sense of mystery, loathsomeness, and separation from the everyday world, yet remain a realistic site for a grand hotel. And as this is a Gothic tale, the abbey needed to have the feel of something old and forgotten, a place given over to memory that just might be home to spirits. It is hidden away, beyond the everyday, out of touch and out of sight, yet not out of thought. For it is from those attributes that real Gothic horror comes, all the more terrible for being removed from the immediate senses.

While the Maine coast is certainly a real place, neither Winterbay nor the abbey of that name is real. You will not find either on a map, and there are no satellite photos of the abbey's ruins. The story may have originally been based on a list of the most haunted places in America, but we wanted our own unique site that we could embellish and populate with our own nightmares. Thus we crafted Winterbay to feel *real*, rather than adopting an actual location.

You may have also noticed a lack of the gore that has become so prominent in modern horror, often a visceral substitute for more emotional, or spiritual terror. Much of what makes Gothic horror so timeless is the use of psychological fear, which has an impact that extends far beyond floods of blood and simple shock. Stephen Mallatrat, who adapted Susan Hill's ghost novel *The Woman in Black* for the stage, sums up this idea: "Darkness is a powerful ally of terror; something that's glimpsed in a corner is far more frightening than if it's fully observed."

In the hands of the old masters of classic Gothic fiction, the frights really do come more from suggestion. There is terror just beyond reach but right over your shoulder, crouching behind a locked door, or lurking in the dank, dark cellar, it flees before detection. Sanity is also drawn into question. Are these horrors real? In many of the old tales, readers must decide for themselves if the ghosts are actual or wild imaginings. Gothic, at least in its finest sense, is subtle. Ghosts rarely appear to crowds, saving their haunts for lone travelers or lost, broken people, damaged by life and the least equipped to deal with their fears. The reader, like the protagonist, is left to wonder, and fear, all alone.

We hope that the shadows in dark corners of your reading space came alive for you as you read *Winterbay Abbey*.

ACKNOWLEDGMENTS

Many people work to bring a book alive. Without a team, *Winterbay* never would have come to be.

First, let us both thank those who contributed so much to this book. Logan Denmark, you whipped *Winterbay* into shape from that first draft. You've helped Davonna so much in the past, and we're so grateful for your assistance and expertise on this manuscript. You are a story-logic maven! Bernadette Martonick, all your comments really aided us in amping up the storyline, including tweaking Will's interior monologue. Andrew Ernst, thank you so much for your fast read-through and for proofreading. You were an enormous help in getting the book ready for final editing, and we're so glad you loved the story. Leslie Lane, our expert architecture advisor, you really rescued us with those small details that made Will a living, breathing architect. So happy to have had all of you as our first official readers!

Scarlett Rugers, as always you are definitely hair and makeup for a manuscript. Thanks for making *Winterbay* red-carpet ready. We fell in love with your concept design for the cover.

You really understand how to visualize a book, and Davonna was so happy to be working with you again. And kudos to Jason Anderson for his eye-catching design work on the ebook. Jim Whiting, what can we say? As always your edits and suggestions never fail to impress. *Winterbay* shines because of your polishing, and it's been an educational and wonderful experience working with you again. We look forward to collaborating on the next manuscript.

And now for our individual thanks.

Davonna:
A big thanks to John Bladek for encouraging me for so many years to keep writing stories and embarking with me on this journey to co-write a Gothic ghost novel. Andrew Ernst, thanks again for all your support and encouragement on this project. I was so excited for you to read the book the whole time we were writing it! Mom and Dad, thank you so much for taking me to Disneyland all the time when I was a kid and for supporting my career. Your nurturing along with all the amusement park trips really helped foster my imagination. You've always encouraged me to pursue the arts, and as I've gotten older, I've realized this is a true blessing. Not everyone receives this kind of support. Love you both so much!

John:
Thanks, Davonna Juroe, for coming up with so many great ideas, double for being a writer, and for cutting out all my "buts." To Mom and Dad, thanks for being pretty lax about not letting me watch too many scary shows as a kid.

And last, to all of you readers, a big thanks for picking up *Winterbay Abbey*. Writers are here to entertain and offer escapism. Without you and your support there is no one to entertain.

Thanks again, everyone!

ABOUT THE AUTHORS

Davonna Juroe loves ghost stories…as long as they're not *too* scary. She tends toward an overactive imagination and startles easily, making her wonder why she's writing ghostly tales. When she's not drinking tea and writing spooky novels, she's exploring old buildings or daydreaming about her next 80s-inspired Halloween costume. Besides reading and writing full-time, she can also be found taking photos of all things whimsical and fantasy-inspired in parks throughout the Pacific Northwest. Davonna currently lives in Seattle, Washington, home of the famous and magical Troll Bridge.

Winterbay Abbey is Davonna's third book. She is also the author of the Amazon-bestselling young adult novel *Scarlette*, a dark retelling of *Little Red Riding Hood* set in France. Davonna is currently working on *Origin*, a supernatural pop-science novel about the existence of mermaids. To learn more about Davonna and her books, visit her website at http://www.davonnajuroe.com/

John Bladek grew up in Washington State (named for a dead president, but unfortunately not haunted by him). He's always been fascinated by scary stories. The first story he can remember reading on his own was called *Spook's Bones*, a tale of two boys who grant a ghost's last wish to have his bones properly buried, and then enjoy sandwiches in celebration. He also liked listening to ghost stories on the radio and sneaking into the basement on Friday nights to watch the scary TV show, *Ghost Story*, which his mom did not approve of. Every day on his way home from school in 3rd grade, he visited a haunted house. Since then, John has stopped hiding under his pillow when listening to spooky stories, but he still enjoys a good scare. To fuel his cravings, John earned a PhD in History, where all ghosts come from. He loves to play trivia and wonders why he doesn't run into haunted houses anymore.

John's other books include the humorous middle-grade adventure, *Roll up the Streets!* (Kane Miller, 2010) and the funny ghost story, *Lost in Ghostville* (Capstone, 2016). You can learn more about his writing at his blog, http://johnbladek.blogspot.com/

More from Author Davonna Juroe

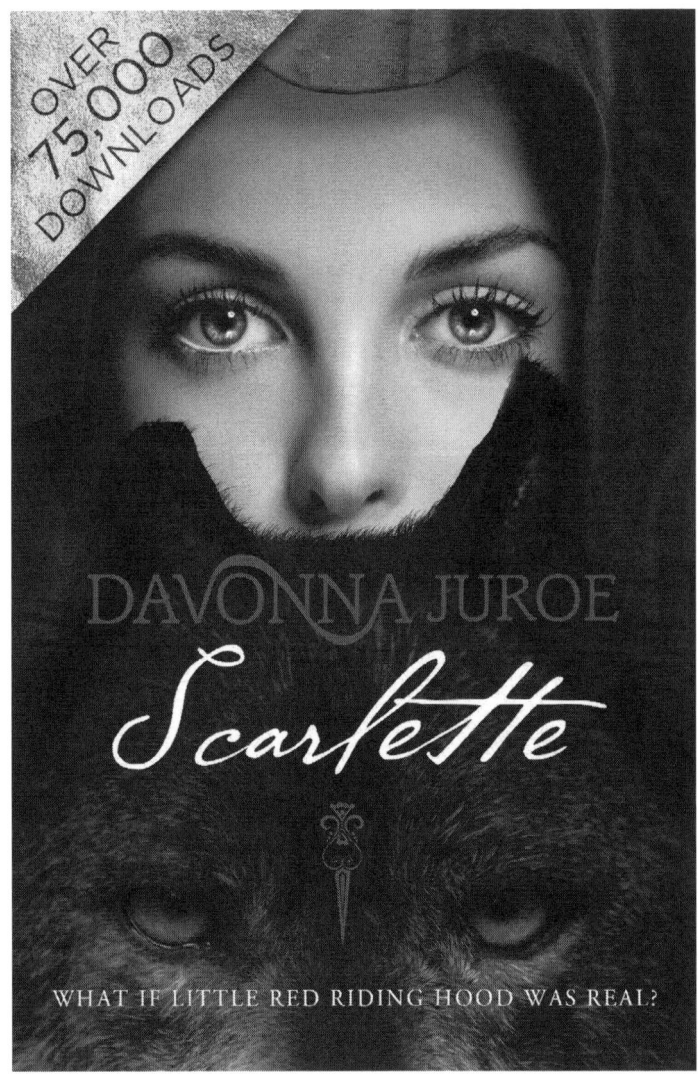

Read on for the first three chapters and Author's Note from *Scarlette*, a dark historical novel that retells "Little Red Riding Hood".

What Readers Are Saying About *Scarlette*...

"Davonna Juroe's *Scarlette* is a captivating retelling of "Little Red Riding Hood." But it is much more than that. Folk tale, historical fiction, and gothic romance all blend harmoniously in this dark and suspenseful novel. The characters are compelling and complex. The plot will keep you guessing until the very end. **The story is beautifully written. With all this in mind, I suspect that Davonna Juroe could be a long-lost Brontë sister.**"
- Jeremy C. Shipp, Bram Stoker Award-nominated author of Cursed, Vacation, *and* Sheep and Wolves

"Well, I love a good mystery, and while *Scarlette* is a Paranormal Historical YA, it holds a fine mystery at its core! And while I'm quite good at guessing, there were twists I did not see coming at all. This novel, in fact, hit all its categories with punch and style. **The paranormal kept me reading at night (even though I should have read it only during daylight hours!); it had a wonderful wealth of historical detail and richness; and it blossomed with the kind of romance completely appropriate for a YA audience.**"
- Kathy Dunnehoff, Amazon best-selling author of The Do-Over

"**This book is a page turner.** As a playwright, I crave true action and drama. This novel has it!"
- Lavonne Mueller, playwright and author

"This is the best book I've read in a long time! ...**It's been forever since I stayed up all night to finish a book. Davonna Juroe can write a mean story, one that I couldn't put down....**"
- *Catherine Schmidt, library technician, Flathead County (Montana) Library*

"***Scarlette* hooked me from the first sentence and kept me spellbound until** *La Fin*.... Promising new author Davonna Juroe has created a living, breathing world with characters so real they could walk off the page....I devoured this must-read book in under twenty-four hours, and I will continue to suffer from symptoms of withdrawal until her next book is released."
- *Hurricane Tyler, fantasy author of* "Requiem for a Steampunk Dream"

Becoming Little Red Riding Hood: Author's Note

"Little Red Riding Hood" is as old as the hills. We all know the story: girl in a red cloak goes into the forest to visit grandma's house, girl is accosted by a wolf posing as Little Red's grandma while hiding in her bed, woodcutter saves Ms. Hood and grandma by slaying the wolf.

What you just read is the widely recognized summary of the Brothers Grimm story printed in Germany in 1857. However, there are many different versions of the tale that predate the Grimms'. One rendition can even be traced all the way to Asia, in which a tiger replaces the villainous wolf.

What's even less known is that many of these alternate versions are far darker than the Brothers' rendering. In fact, the Grimms' is a watered-down take on a parable-like story first printed at the end of the 17th century. *Tales of Mother Goose*, written by French aristocrat Charles Perrault, contains retellings of older folk tales such as "Cinderella," "Blue Beard," "Puss in Boots," "Sleeping Beauty," and of course "Little Red Riding Hood."

I was surprised that Perrault's work was not the tame Grimm story I'd grown up with. Told as a cautionary tale warning young women of men's "wolfish" appetites, it was aimed at the promiscuous courtiers of the French Court. Modern readers are often shocked by Perrault's tragic end for the heroine. There is no woodcutter to save Red Riding Hood. Instead, she undresses, climbs into bed, and is killed by the wolf who "devours" her. Interestingly, during Perrault's time, the common euphemism for a woman who'd lost her virginity was that she "had been with the wolf."

Perrault's slant struck a chord with me, and I decided to adopt an overall similarly dark mood for *Scarlette*. However, I did not want to completely dismiss the Grimms' elements. Many of their details, such as the woodcutter, found their way into the novel. These aspects were then blended with historical events to give the fairy tale an authentic realism.

The other feature I had hoped to capture was the naiveté and poor judgment of Little Red Riding Hood as a character. Some of Riding Hood's decisions are almost comical. In one scene, she actually shows the sly wolf the way to her grandmother's woodland house. Even more baffling, is her obliviousness to the dog-like qualities of her "sick" grandmother as the wolf. She remains frustratingly blind throughout both the Grimm and the Perrault versions.

The reader will find nods to this baffling gullibility throughout *Scarlette*. However, as guileless as Scarlette's character seems at times, she is not a completely ignorant nineteen-year-old. Taught by her grandmother to read at a young age, Scarlette takes advantage of a rare educational opportunity that was almost unheard of in Old Regime France.

It was a tough world all around for a peasant in that era. The novel depicts some of the harsh realities such as poverty and hunger within the Gévaudan province. *Scarlette* also revolves around the infamous and horrific Beast of Gévaudan attacks of the 1760s. Fittingly, the Beast provided a convincing substitute for the wolf from "Little Red Riding Hood."

One historical component not portrayed in *Scarlette*, however, is the language of the era. While little writing by peasants still exists, a middle-class 18th century journeyman named Jacques-Louis Ménétra wrote a journal. I familiarized myself with his writing but decided early on that I didn't want to utilize his style or precise language. Rather, I wanted the novel to remain accessible to a modern audience unfamiliar with 18th century French, even in translation. So the common language of today functions as a stand-in for the common language of yesteryear.

Some historical fiction buffs may consider this a risky move. One wants to be as historically accurate as possible, but I believe that, after consulting author and history Ph.D. John Bladek, he accurately describes the historical fiction dilemma:

The noun in the phrase 'historical fiction' is fiction. Historical is an adjective describing it, but in no way does that make 'fiction' into 'history'.

Is there any real difference between writing something about the present that's made-up versus writing something about the past that's made-up? Time is relative.

Putting a more formal version of English into the mouths of French peasants from the 18th century is no more historical than having Romeo and Juliet—two Italian teens—speak via

Shakespeare in the finest English poetry ever written. It may feel authentic, but that comes from the mistaken impression by many that formal language always portrays the past in a more authentic manner. There is little justification for this belief.

There are no sound recordings from the 18th century, so we simply do not know how people spoke. And there is scant justification for putting the more formal writing of the period into the mouths of peasants.

Having French peasants speak like educated Englishmen is a bit far-fetched as well. And considering that Scarlette *is a contemporary young adult novel, the answer as to what language was appropriate for the readership seemed obvious.*

Other "modernized" historical fiction has followed these ideas, including Suzannah Dunn's *The Sixth Wife*, which is set during the reign of England's Edward VI. *A Knight's Tale*, while a film, is also another clear example of modern language used in a period piece.

Blending contemporary language, Gothic Romance elements, history, and fairy tale into *Scarlette* was no easy task. I made thousands of executive storytelling decisions to fit the novel's demands. What you are about to read is a new historical reimagining of "Little Red Riding Hood." One that is my contribution to the evolution of the fairy tale and an homage to the girl behind the red cloak.

"Love is blind; therefore, it loves the dark."
-Tadeusz Gicgier

MARGARIDE MOUNTAINS, GÉVAUDAN PROVINCE, FRANCE

JUNE 1767

Fear. Panic. Anxiety.

Mother was like a bloodhound. Smelling the air, she could sense my feelings, and any whiff of unease set her at my throat.

If I didn't stop having these painful emotions around her, I would surely lose my freedom.

We were like the moon and the sun, she and I. We could never be close, but I had no idea our lives were about to collide.

CHAPTER ONE

One Month Earlier

I glanced over my shoulder at the black forest. The knots in my stomach loosened when I saw that the boulder-lined road snaking westward towards the misted woods was empty.

I faced forward, breathing easier, but still couldn't shake the fear. Our limestone cottage came into view, nestled between the granite ravines under the rock-columned cliffs. No smoke wafted from the chimney, and the sheep pen was empty. Mother wasn't back from the pastures yet, and we needed to get home before her.

I put my arm around Grandma's shoulders to steady her. Her leg seemed worse than usual, and she ambled more slowly than she had on our way out to gather roots and berries.

"Don't worry, Scarlette. We'll be there soon," Grandma said, as wisps of her breath puffed from her lips.

I wrapped my shawl tighter, fighting the chill, and tried to smile. But Grandma's words couldn't keep me from worrying about Mother, or about being this close to the forest.

Peasants and villagers alike were told not to venture beyond the tree line. It wasn't safe. The townspeople were leaving their houses less and less. Even traveling merchants stopped visiting our province.

Many of us couldn't afford necessities anymore. Some even remained in bed because they didn't have money for clothing. We were all trapped by the surrounding forest, and the town was becoming a wasteland of graves.

So many people had been found buried in the underbrush with their throats shredded. Other horrifying tales flew around the village. But it was these grisly stories that gained so much attention, and it was becoming impossible to separate truth from superstition.

Grandma and I were sure the attacks were only a wolf's doing. There were no such things as supernatural creatures. But many villagers insisted it was the *loup-garou*, a werewolf. Perhaps most sinister was that almost everyone suspected one another. Many spent their days seeking signs that their neighbor could be transforming into a wolf.

The growing paranoia led to all sorts of awful practices. The worst being to scatter hunks of meat sprinkled with wolfsbane throughout our lands in the hope of warding off the predator. I didn't know if this herb's "magical" abilities could stop werewolves, but the poisonous leaves had killed many of the poor scavenging for scraps. After two years of early frosts killing our crops, I couldn't blame them for looking. But it had been three years of attacks, and the strewn meat bits obviously weren't working. It was a waste of good food, and that was all the more reason for me to despise superstition. It was responsible for too many unnecessary deaths.

I felt better knowing that the attacks never happened during the day. But even when there was daylight, we never knew if the darkness of the woods hid the wolf among the brush, masking its next move.

Although Mother had forbidden us from ever going near the forest, Grandma, Mother, and I needed food. Even if it meant skirting the woods. One crust of bread couldn't last us for the rest of the month. Grandma and I picked whatever roots and scant berries we could find a short distance from the tree line.

But even being only close to the forest was enough to keep me on pins and needles. We had our bladed staffs, but I wished the law hadn't forbade peasants from bearing arms. Blades didn't offer the protection a pistol could.

Grandma mentioned we should gather the flowers today. But we both knew this was unthinkable. Even though it was our favorite tradition, and one small thread of joy we could share in this dark shrouded life, we couldn't take the risk.

I loved the poppy bouquets Grandma made for my birthday. Although I knew I was getting too old for them, they made a beautiful crown. But three years ago Mother found out about us gathering flowers in our favorite clearing, and I didn't want to have a repeat of that miserable day. I could almost feel Mother's nails scraping my skin again.

Somehow Grandma was able to calm Mother's violent temper that afternoon. Luckily I never had any physical contact with Mother after that horrid day. But from then on, my name permanently changed from "You" to "Wretch." Sometimes I really think if it weren't for Grandma, I wouldn't know my real name.

Mother's fits became worse after she "christened" me. And her favorite activity seemed to be chasing me down into a gauntlet of torment. Many times I caught her spitting in my soup. Another time I saw her put filth in my bed like I was some pig sleeping in a pen. Grandma never saw any of this. I knew I could tell her anything, but I didn't want to burden her with all of my woes. Instead I would save my secrets and tears for my trips to the village well. Whenever I lowered the water bucket down the shaft, I would wish that somehow we could all be a happy family. Where the smiles outnumbered the frowns. I didn't understand why Mother couldn't love Grandma or me.

My wishes never came true and, more and more, I realized I couldn't defend Grandma or myself. Mother seemed determined to provoke me. But I couldn't take her bait and rouse her anger, or the authorities would be at our door. I wasn't sure how she got the *lettres de catchet*, as peasants rarely possessed them. These documents—authorized by the King— let families lock up "unruly" relatives. It would take just one word and Grandma and I would be separated forever.

I had to bear everything.

Alone.

But somehow Grandma caught on to Mother's secret cruelties. She said nothing at first, but I noticed she would clean my bed or sweep around it. She smiled her crescent-moon grin, and said she was just "tidying up." I knew better. "Tidying up" meant "You're not alone."

That day, I promised Grandma I would never leave her alone either.

I was pulled from my thoughts when I heard Grandma's breathing become more labored. "Must…rest." She stopped and leaned against a granite boulder, laid down her bladed oak staff, and hunched over her knees.

"Grandma, please. We're almost there," I said, my voice rising. "If I don't start supper before Mother…"

She looked up at me. Her eyes, blueberry in color, were serene, hypnotic. So many times I'd thought nothing would ever be right again. But with that one gaze, my frosty blizzards melted into balmy midsummer afternoons.

She reached up and put her calloused hands on my cheeks. Her touch could calm a condemned man standing at the gallows. Star-white stray locks fell from her tattered cream cap over her forehead, caressing her soft wrinkled face. "I'll be fine.

Go on. I have this. See?" She picked up her staff and brandished it like a knight about to slay a dragon.

I couldn't help but laugh.

"I'll be right behind you. These old legs just can't rush anymore."

"No, let me just help you."

I moved forward to steady her, but she winced as she hobbled on her bad leg. She shook her head. "I need rest. Don't worry. I can see the cottage from here, and I'll see your mother on the road if she comes. When I spot the sheep, I'll duck down behind one of the boulders so she won't see me. Then I'll tell her a story about going to the well." She patted my hand. "If you don't leave now, she'll find out, and then where will we be?"

My mind split. I didn't feel good about leaving her, but I could see our cottage door. It was still daylight. Grandma wouldn't have far to go.

"Trust me," she said.

"All right." I sighed. "I hate you having to lie."

Grandma smiled, kissed me on my nose, and winked. "Sometimes we need to lie to protect our happiness."

I took her wrinkled hand and squeezed it.

She brushed some dust off her frayed white dress and apron. As she handed me her basket of berries and roots, she said, "Try to relax. If your mother asks where we got these, we can tell her that Jeanne picked them."

I smiled, thanking God for Jeanne. She was the only friend I could turn to for help. And she was good at keeping secrets.

Secrets. Would I never be rid of them?

"Scarlette, look at me."

I stared into Grandma's eyes.

"One day you and I will live together in a castle and do whatever we please," Grandma said. "Now hurry. But first, give me a smile."

I grinned. "All right, I'll see you in a moment," I said and ran towards the cottage.

The road ahead, which led east towards the village, was empty. Looking over my shoulder, I felt some comfort seeing Grandma wave. But I froze when I reached our door. The sound of bleating sheep echoed off the gorge's walls.

Mother.

CHAPTER TWO

I rushed inside, slid the food baskets underneath my bed, and lit the cooking fire. I didn't want to have to explain about the berries, roots, and Grandma's absence all at the same time. As I stood over the pot, tossing in old bread scraps, my hands shook. When the water began to boil, I heard the snap of the sheep-pen gate. I whisked the gruel, pretending everything was normal. I hoped Grandma had been able to duck down in time.

The door flew open and Mother stepped into our one-room cottage, bladed staff in hand. A gust of damp spring air wafted inside. Goosebumps scaled on my arms as the heat from the cooking fire escaped out the door, along with my hope for a peaceful supper. Avoiding her iron-gray eyes, I tried to control my fear.

She slammed the door, and the cottage shook. I winced as a piece of thatch fell from the ceiling onto the dirt floor. Dull light peeked through a tiny hole in the crisscrossed straw roof. I sighed. I would have to fix that. God knows she wouldn't. And there was no point asking her to be careful. She could make anything my fault: a lost sheep, her muddy shoes, or even a bad frost. And the last thing I wanted to hear right now was blame for a shabby roof.

"*Salut*," I said, as I stoked the flames under the pot. I stepped back, waving away ashen smoke, and poured myself a cup of water. Trying to hide my worry, I asked, "Would you like some, Mother?" Carefully, I put another cup on the table.

I took a sip and darted my eyes towards the tiny window. The beginning wisps of a spring fog crept down the ravine walls. I didn't see Grandma. Where was she? Was she still resting?

Mother muttered something about the good-for-nothing soldiers not doing their jobs. "Found another girl dead, they did, out there among the trees. Serves her right. Nothing natural comes of that forest. Soldiers will never find that beast, lazy criminals." She pointed at me. "I'd better never catch you going out there."

I swallowed as I put my cup on the table and walked back to the pot.

"And supper better be done soon. I've got chapel tonight. *Someone* must pray for our souls."

I clenched the soup spoon and stirred harder. I didn't need to be reminded about how she went to chapel every night to pray for my soul—and *everyone* else's.

Out of the corner of my eye, I watched her lean her staff against the limestone wall. As she turned toward me, I stole a glance at her. Her bloodshot eyes and weathered face gave her the appearance of someone at least twice her age. Grandma always said that Mother used to be cheerful and a beauty like Aphrodite. Looking at her now, I couldn't see how. To me, Mother had always seemed like sour milk. And over the years both her looks and her temper had continued to spoil.

"What're you looking at?" Mother snapped while opening her satchel.

I didn't answer, but watched her place a package of meat and a bouquet of purple wolfsbane on the table. I couldn't believe her. Clearly, she'd been to town to buy these items. That meant she'd left the sheep to fend for themselves, and we couldn't afford—

"Grind up the plant and put it on the meat when you're done," she said.

I frowned. "But we could eat—"

"Do as you're told, wretched girl." She hung up her gray cloak and pulled off her taupe linen cap. Dirt brown hair fell to her elbows.

I watched the porridge boil, trying to hold my tongue.

"I mean now," she said, her voice rising.

I picked up the meat package, but the bloody shank slipped out of my fingers. I gasped.

"What's wrong with you? Pick that up!" she yelled, pointing to the beef. "Worthless."

Brushing off as much dirt as I could, I put the chunk back on the table, but pricked my thumb on a splinter. "Ow," I cried, sucking the salty blood.

"Look at you. Thumb in your mouth like a babe." Mother shook her head. "Useless like your grandmother. Where is that old cow anyway?"

My cheeks warmed. I looked out the window at the chestnut tree in front of the cottage. Its fading shadow had bent and twisted far to the right. The day was dying. Something was wrong. Had she fallen?

Waiting for an answer, Mother glared at me.

I kept my eyes down. "She's out fetching water."

She grabbed my water cup from the table and threw it on the floor. "I just passed by the well."

"Then, she must have..." I wrung my hands, trying to think of something to say, "taken another way home. I'll go look for her."

I stepped toward the threshold to open the door. But Mother put out her arm, blocking my exit. I looked into her eyes. Black shadows hung low under her lashes, and a pox mark dented her cheek like a thumbprint pressing into the skin of an apple.

"You're hiding something from me," she said, pointing to my face.

"No, I… I'm not. I'm just hungry, and I want to find Grandma so we can eat."

"You'll be lucky if the door is unlatched when you get back." She took papers from her apron pocket and waved them in my face.

Locking her threatening words into my blackened chest of memories, I looked outside. Even the darkening skies and gloomy haze seemed more inviting than being in a warm cottage with Mother. She put the *lettres* back in her pocket and dropped her arm.

A quick sigh of relief escaped my lips. I wiped my hands on my apron and stepped outside into the cool evening air. As the wind picked up, my goosebumps reappeared. This reminded me that I needed my cloak. But there was no way I was going back inside.

I strode into the cutting breeze and walked a little ways towards the village. When Mother closed the door, I backtracked and ran west towards the withering sunlight.

CHAPTER THREE

My throat tightened as I reached the boulder where I'd left Grandma.

Gone.

Trying to stop my hands from shaking, I glanced back towards our cottage and down the road.

She couldn't have passed the house. I would've seen or heard her. I scanned the tree line, but there was no sign of her. Where was she?

Running towards the trees, I hoped to retrace our footsteps and fight the panic crawling through my stomach. My mind kept flipping through possible explanations of what had happened. But all I could think of was the wolf. Hoping to calm myself, I tried to think of any possible reasons why she wasn't in sight. Perhaps she thought to get more food, or maybe she walked to our neighbor Bernard's to get out of the cold. But her hurt leg. She couldn't have gone too far.

Almost at the tree line, I saw Bernard's cottage. Rusted gardening tools lay scattered on the soil, and the awning sagged horribly, making the windows and doors look like a crestfallen mouth and eyes. Swaying in the slight breeze, dried braids of garlic and wolfsbane hung from the porch beams, while puffs of blue-gray smoke pulsed from the chimney.

It'd been a month since the latest wolf attack, and that was the last time I'd seen anyone come out of that house. A memory of Bernard carrying his wife Odette from the forest, innards ripped, flashed before my eyes. Odette's screams rang throughout the village, just as the screams of the dozens before her had. I tried to push the scene from my head to stop the sickening feeling growing in my belly.

I didn't want to intrude on him, but I had no choice.

I was almost at his cottage, when something caught my eye. My head pounded. Up ahead, a white apron lay rumpled in the middle of the path. As I ran to pick it up, I noticed a fresh blood stain near the hem. I glanced down, and my neck hair stood up. Fingernail markings raked the dirt, leaving a trail into the woods.

Without thinking, I ran towards the forest.

When I stepped inside the woods, the canopy turned the dusk into blackness. Now shivering, I could see the ghostly haze from my breath. In the distance, shorter pine trees arched over the path, creating a tunnel of green needles. Grandma was nowhere in sight, and I began to run faster to raise my body temperature and my courage.

Please be all right. Please be all right. What have I done? Why did I leave her? Sweat dewed up on my forehead despite the cold.

"Grandma?" I called into the forest. The only reply was the crunching of pine needles under my wooden shoes.

I didn't have much further to go when my nightmare sharpened. Lying halfway on the road and halfway in the grass was a broken oak staff. Next to the splintered wood, a trail of broken branches snaked into the underbrush.

My hands trembled as I picked up the bladed half of the staff. I ran through the bushes. The shrubs were becoming thicker, but I stopped when I heard something.

The sound of brush being parted and loud cracks of thick branches splitting shot a bullet of fear into my heart. Only something with enormous weight could make that much noise.

I held up the staff and squinted through the darkness, but couldn't make out where the sound was coming from. "Hello? Grandma?" I called.

Whatever it was, it was picking up speed and crashing through the brush. My breath became shallow and rapid, and I put my hand on a thick tree trunk to steady myself. Another branch snapped. This time it came from behind me.

I spun around, and my mouth dropped. A woman lay on top of a bed of gnarled roots. Entwined within her dirty silver hair were twigs and leaves. Bloodstains soiled her arms and face.

**

End of this sample book. Enjoyed the sample?

Buy *Scarlette* on Amazon.com.